the girl
who
would
be
russian

also by willis johnson

the year of the longley

the girl
who
would
be
russian

and other stories

willis johnson

HARCOURT BRACE JOVANOVICH, PUBLISHERS
San Diego   New York   London

Requests for permission to make copies of any part of the work should be mailed to: Permissions, Harcourt Brace Jovanovich, Publishers, Orlando, Florida 32887.

The story "Prayer for the Dying" first appeared in TriQuarterly, Fall 1982, pp. 23–37. It was reprinted in The Pushcart Prize VIII, edited by Bill Henderson (Wainscott, N.Y.: The Pushcart Press, 1984), and in Prize Stories: The O. Henry Awards 1984, edited by William Abrahams (New York: Doubleday & Co., 1984). "The Ice Fish" first appeared in Yale Review, Summer 1983, pp. 541–560. It was reprinted in Inside Vacationland: New Fiction from the Real Maine, edited by Mark Melnicove (South Harpswell, Me.: The Dog Ear Press, 1985). "The Girl Who Would Be Russian" first appeared in Southern Review, Winter 1985, pp. 144–161.

Library of Congress Cataloging-in-Publication Data
Johnson, Willis, 1938–
    The girl who would be Russian and other stories.
    Contents: The Great Valentinova — The ice fish — Prayer for the dying [etc.]
    1. Russian Americans—Maine—Fiction. I. Title.
PS3560.03868G5 1986   813'.54   85–24765
ISBN 0–15–135691–2

Designed by Francesca M. Smith
Printed in the United States of America
First edition
A B C D E

To Christine

contents

the
great
valentinova

Marietta Valentinova, the famous ballerina who lived over the hardware store, was peeking through the faded curtain at the audience gathered for her annual Winter Gala Ballet. Under her coat she was wearing a dancing costume padded to make her look like an egg, for Moussorgsky's "Ballet of the Unhatched Chicks," her opening number. Before a performance Marietta Valentinova was always tense and frequently snapped at people. Today it was more than nerves. A muscle throbbed in her jaw. Her red lips were pressed together so tightly you could see behind them the outline of her teeth. Mr. Farley, who was standing in the wing with the curtain rope in his big freckled hands, started to get scared.

Mr. Farley was the custodian. The ballerina was already cross with him because when she'd arrived with her costumes and record player, the hall was locked. She found him across the street in the kitchen of the Hotel Nicholas the Second, where he had been given a cup of coffee for shoveling the walk. Then she yelled because, when he let her in, the fire wasn't going. A big blue vein bulged in the middle of her forehead. The ballerina was just a tiny thing but when she yelled it made you afraid.

Except for the loud yawns of the Golikov girl selling tickets at the card table by the door, the people in the hall were silent. The wood was snapping in the stove but the heat hadn't reached the audience yet. Through the side of the curtain Mr. Farley could see various people looking down at their watches and repositioning themselves on the icy metal chairs. They read the Pledge of Allegiance to Jesus, which the Methodist ladies had embroidered on a big piece of cloth and tacked to the wall. They looked up at the bare light bulbs suspended over their heads like drops of water that had frozen after leaking through the ceiling. They were all still wearing hats and coats. The minister, the Reverend Mr. McFarland, sat beside the ballerina's record player, blowing into his plump hands. In the front row, three high-backed chairs remained empty. These the ballerina had had Mr. Farley set out for the baroness and her husband, Maxim Maximovich, and for Father Alexey, the priest of the Church of Vasily the Blessed. They were the leading citizens of the Russian community so their seats were right in the middle.

Marietta Valentinova snapped the curtain shut. She stalked off the stage, her small hands fists. "Five minutes," she said to the balalaika player and Sofya Andreyevna, who used to sing in cabarets. They were to perform during the ballerina's costume changes. Marietta Valentinova pulled her coat collar up around her neck. Thick wool stockings covered her legs. "Five minutes, then priest or no priest—baroness and her half-professor can cook in hell—we are starting. After all, I am a professional. You, can't you do something with that wretched fire?"

"She's banked full," said Mr. Farley. The hard way she looked at him made him blink.

"Then I suggest you make it fuller—if you don't mind."

"I don't mind." Mr. Farley's feet worked under him a little, but he stayed in place.

"Well?"

"I thought I was supposed to do the curtain."

The ballerina closed her eyes. "First the fire," she said in a very controlled way. "Then the curtain."

Mr. Farley looked uncertain. He began to fidget. His fingers did a stiff little dance on the legs of his trousers.

"Go on," Sofya Andreyevna assured him. "We won't start without you."

Reluctantly, he left. Mr. Farley liked being around Russians, even when they got mad and yelled. Before they came, nothing much ever happened in the town. Once in a while some fool would drink too much and get himself shot in a hunting camp or at the mobile home park. In the spring the river would flood, and sometimes under the bridge, stuck in one of the pilings, they'd find a patient from the State Hospital who'd jumped in upstream. Mostly, people in town kept quiet and to themselves, kept whatever it was that they were behind the doors of their tall, sedate wooden houses, living and dying that way without anyone ever knowing what went on inside.

But Russians—they did things right out in the open where you could see and hear even if you couldn't exactly understand. They had three churches in town, one for the upper-class Russians, one for the Ukrainians, and one for the rest of them. Once there was a big fight outside the door of the high-class church over whom it belonged to legally, the Union of True Russians, which owned the building, or the congregation. For a long time afterwards there were rumors of conspiracies and even of the Communists somehow being behind it. But the next thing you knew, the people of the church were all together again eating cabbage rolls and *pirozhki* in honor of one of their saints, only sitting as far as possible from the ones they had fought with this time, which in some cases put them next to the ones they had fought with the last time. The Russians held the suppers for their saints in the Methodist Church hall because their own churches were too poor to have halls. Mr. Farley, being the custodian, went to every function. Pretty soon they'd start to sing and then some of them, their faces red from the vodka they kept under their tables, would start to dance while others would blow their noses and wipe the tears from their eyes.

Mr. Farley also liked to hang around the Hotel Nicholas the Second, where a lot of the older ones lived, or he'd go downstreet to the store where they bought their groceries and watch them come in and out, jabbering away in their language of which Mr. Farley, try as he might, could not understand one word. When it was Russian Easter, which was almost always at a different time than the Methodist one, Mr. Farley would hear them singing in the middle of the night. He'd put on his trousers and go out, seeing his breath under the street lamps in the cold of the spring night. From the shadows he'd watch as they paraded around their churches with candles stuck through Dixie cups to catch the wax.

In one of their churches they kept a dead man. Mr. Farley had seen him one day when the Reverend Mr. McFarland sent him to borrow chairs for a bean supper the Methodists were having. The priest had not answered the doorbell so Mr. Farley had wandered into the church, the Holy Virgin of Kazan, which in the old days had been a shed for ice-cutting tools. (Vasily the Blessed, the upper-class church, had been a stable, which, its parishioners said, was better than having been a shed and infinitely better than having been a saloon, which the Ukrainian church had been.)

The dead man was lying in the middle of the dark, his face lit by candles, little silver smoke pots set all around him. Faces had glowered at Mr. Farley from the darkness, golden faces and white faces, as white and still as the dead man's, faces with fearful eyes and mournful eyes. Mr. Farley did not stay long.

"Ignorant person!" Marietta Valentinova said after Mr. Farley had gone woefully out the stage door to tend to the fire. She spat as if she had bitten into something moldy. "God knows this place is full of them!"

"Part of the charm," said the balalaika player. His name was Christian, and he was a young man with a beard, new in town. He was an American but he had learned in college how to play the balalaika. Marietta Valentinova had recruited him for her Winter Gala as a hedge against Sofya Andreyevna getting drunk again.

Sofya Andreyevna was seated on the only whole chair to be found among the piles of broken furniture and other

church debris the Reverend Mr. McFarland had stored backstage so he wouldn't have to haul it to the dump. "What's
wrong?" she asked. Her yellow hair sat atop her head like
a hat a size too small. Her nose was a tangle of little blue
and red veins. "What do you expect in the country? This
isn't New Jersey, you know."

Marietta Valentinova had lived in New Jersey before moving to Maine. She had gotten many good write-ups for her
dancing in the newspapers down there. Only the air with
so many factories and automobiles had not been good for
her health.

"I'm sick to death of such charm," she said.

"I'll amend it to 'quaint,' " Christian said.

"And sick to death of the ignorance."

"He's a nice man, the janitor," said Sofya Andreyevna.
"What's wrong with you today?"

"Nothing, Sofya Andreyevna. Absolutely nothing," the
ballerina said. She looked as if she could weep. "The hall is
freezing. Everybody's waiting. This miserable little town."

"Come on, it's not so bad. You're just on edge. Anyway,
we're here."

Marietta Valentinova turned away. It was easy for Sofya
Andreyevna to say that, she thought. Sofya Andreyevna was
old and fat. She wasn't going anyplace anymore. She didn't
even want to. Marietta Valentinova might not be as young
as she used to be, but she wasn't old. Believe it or not, she
still could fit into costumes she wore twenty, thirty years
ago. One day, with all the antipollution devices they were
inventing, the air might become clean enough for her to
return to New Jersey. Or maybe she would move to San
Francisco. She had a cousin in San Francisco. Maybe her
cousin would know of a nice hall she could rent, and she

would present a wonderful ballet that would keep the people of San Francisco talking for years to come. She still had a lot of options.

She took from the pocket of her coat the vial with the pills that calmed her. She got the spit up in her mouth, placed one on the back of her tongue, and swallowed. She crossed herself three times.

When Marietta Valentinova had gone back to the center of the curtain to peek out again at the audience, Sofya Andreyevna turned to the balalaika player and said, "Don't think anything of it. She's always like this when she dances."

"It doesn't bother me," Christian said.

"She says it's Tolstoy's fault. That's right, Tolstoy. Don't laugh, please. She blames him for everything. She says it's because of him that she's here, that we're all here. She even wrote to his daughter in New York. I saw the letter, God help me. This was several years ago. 'Forgive me, Countess,' she said, 'but in my opinion if it wasn't for your father, there would still be a Tsar and a country called Russia and a city called Petersburg and that's where I'd be living right now and dancing in the Maryinski.' The woman didn't answer, of course."

Sofya Andreyevna leaned to one side to see if the ballerina was looking. From her purse she took a thin, silver-colored flask. She unscrewed the top, took a drink from it, and grimaced. Then she took another, longer one.

"It's for my cold," she said to Christian, who smiled.

"What she says," Sofya Andreyevna continued, putting the flask away, "is that he may have been a good writer but he wasn't a very good person—and he definitely wasn't a good Russian, not the way he behaved. He treated his wife miserably. He didn't care for the church or the Tsar or anybody but serfs and other ignorant people. And all of this little by little came out in his books. The next thing you know—revolution."

"Incredible," Christian said.

"Are you laughing? I'm telling you. She's got a whole theory."

"But Tolstoy?"

"Why not? It's somebody's fault, no? Like she says—we're here."

In a little while Marietta Valentinova returned and said, "Well, I'm sorry, but I've waited long enough."

"Give them another minute," Sofya Andreyevna said. "It's Sunday. Maybe the priest got busy."

"My dear Sofya Andreyevna, the service ended hours ago. I don't know why you want to argue all the time. No, we're starting. Please," she said to the balalaika player, "remind the minister we're starting with the Moussorgsky. Where's that stupid man for the curtain?"

Christian was about to go when they heard the outside door rattle and bang. They heard feet stomping off snow.

"Do you mean they haven't started yet?" a loud voice said. It was the baroness. "They must want to make certain everyone is frozen first. Look, you can see your breath!"

There was a small amount of polite, respectful laughter. Many of the people in the audience lived at the Nicholas the Second, which the baroness owned.

Mr. Farley ran back in a clumsy, disjointed way, as if his limbs were too big for the rest of his body to handle. "They're here," he said excitedly.

The ballerina peered out. Father Alexey, entering in the baroness's wake like a dinghy in tow, went to the front of the hall and blessed the audience. On a chain around his neck there was a large cross, and he held this aloft over the bowed heads. The priest had a long beard and thin hair tied at the back of his head in a limp little tail. The old women in town worried that he was much too thin and pasty-looking. "You've got to eat more, *batyushka*," they'd tell him. He was a monk and he lived alone in a couple of rooms in the old house next to the church.

The baroness stood erect at the priest's side, surveying the audience like a general, her bosom thrust forward like artillery shells. On her handsome face was her more or less permanent look of disapproval. Her narrow nostrils were lifted as if she smelled something unpleasant. Her husband, a tall man with a clipped mustache and a small ironic smile, stood with his mouth wiggling as if he were drawing spit. Maxim Maximovich was in the real estate business. He prided himself on being the father of the colony since it had been his advertisements in the Russian-language newspapers in New York and San Francisco that had brought the first Russians to town. Nearly everyone had bought his house or farm or found his rental through Maxim Maximovich, or else lived in his wife's hotel. Some people called him the half-professor, the title deriving from the fact that although he taught some real estate courses at the community college in Augusta, he was not a full professor.

At the end of his prayer, Father Alexey crossed himself with a large, devout gesture and the people crossed themselves, some large and devout, others small and quick. The Reverend Mr. McFarland switched off the lights. Although it was still afternoon, the room fell dark. The thin winter daylight pressed feebly against the windowpanes as if it did not have the strength to enter. Christian tiptoed over to make sure the minister knew about the Moussorgsky. The Reverend Mr. McFarland blew the fuzz off the needle.

Marietta Valentinova's expression was suddenly lofty and

serene, as if she had ascended to a place above the cold hall, above the dust and broken furniture. Behind her on the backstage floor her woolen stockings lay like empty cocoons. On her feet was a pair of dainty red shoes.

"The curtain, Mr. Farley," she said.

She danced the whole of the Moussorgsky up on her toes. She did not try anything more strenuous than a few pirouettes. Marietta Valentinova detested gymnastics on the stage. As she often told Sofya Andreyevna, anyone could gallop about and leap into the air. Also the egg costume, which she herself had designed, was a bit restrictive. In any case, an unhatched chick—she imagined its little red legs stuck through the shell—was just getting its feet on the ground, so to speak, and wasn't going to be jumping all over the place.

What she gave an audience, she felt, was something else, something beautiful. God only knew, it was something the town, with its two streets and plastic flowers in the window boxes, did not have in abundance. The river in summer could be nice but in dry spells it often became a flat brown stream between muddy banks. The woods, though deep and green, were filled with mosquitoes and black flies. Some days the air was fresh but on others you could smell the chicken barns being cleaned out after the flocks had been hauled off to the packing plant. And there was absolutely no culture, not even a movie house. All there was to do was go to the store or the laundromat or sit in the hotel lobby and watch the old people creaking up the stairs to their solitary rooms. Perhaps it was vain to think and vain to say but the ballerina had to say it: Thank God for herself! Thank God for the little light she brought each winter, bright and rare and gemlike, into the dismal life of the town. Without her there would be almost nothing, certainly not beauty and certainly not grace. When the dance ended, Mr. Farley closed the curtain before Marietta Valentinova had a chance to take her bow. She pawed her way out between the folds. As she bowed she saw under her brows the guests of honor nodding their approval. She rose blowing kisses. As she skipped off the stage, her happy look vanished only long enough for her to throw Mr. Farley a fierce glare. Sofya Andreyevna and the balalaika player were clapping for her. The ballerina squeezed the old singer's fat hands. They exchanged proximity kisses near one another's rouged cheeks.

"Well, now me," said Sofya Andreyevna, and she went out on the stage.

Marietta Valentinova retired behind a blackboard, which once had been used for Sunday school. She had had Mr. Farley roll it across one corner of the backstage so she could change without being gawked at by him. It was a large blackboard and it was set on legs whose wheels chirped like birds. The board was the color of smoke from being erased too much without being washed. Still legible across the top were the words WHY I LOVE GOD. Marietta Valentinova could see where a list had been made—she could make out some numbers—but the words were gone.

She removed her egg costume and sat on the lid of a trunk dabbing at the perspiration on her lip and forehead, dropping tissues in wads on the floor. All around her were chairs with missing legs, dusty hymnals with yellow pages, a stained mattress, a cardboard box full of candle ends. Out on the stage Sofya Andreyevna was singing a song, accompanied on the piano by the Reverend Mr. McFarland. The piano was badly out of tune, but then so was Sofya Andreyevna. Marietta Valentinova hardly noticed. She had taken off one of her shoes and was admiring her toes as if they were a set of pearls. Her three middle toes were almost exactly the same length. Perhaps not aristocratic feet, she thought, but priceless ones for a dancer. On point they gave her perfect balance. Pavlova herself would have envied them.

She once had seen Pavlova dance. It was in London, where her family had settled for a while after the Revolution and where Marietta Valentinova was born. She was not sure whether what she remembered was what she had actually seen or what her mother, on whose lap she'd sat during the performance, later told her. A vision she had nonetheless. It was of a lovely creature, perfection in white, gliding on a sea of light, the light its own reflected brilliance. Somewhere in her memory was also the memory of her mother's tears but this too was vague and Marietta Valentinova did not know if her mother had cried in the theater or somewhere else but she liked to think that it was there in the balcony with Pavlova dancing and her mother, true Russian that she was, moved to tears; and those tears and that swan awakening in the child the beauty and the passion and the grace.

Out on the stage, Sofya Andreyevna had finished her song. She was winding up her act with the same anecdote she had told at Marietta Valentinova's last Winter Gala, about a peasant woman who buys a washing machine and gets her breast caught in the wringer.

Marietta Valentinova put on her white chiffon gown. On the wall was a mirror framed with dusty wooden grapes and swirls. She dropped a little spit on a tissue and tried to rub the glass clean but only smeared the dirt. She rubbed at the mirror with another tissue and more spit, but the face that looked back at her remained clouded, indistinct. Marietta Valentinova seemed startled, as if she had only just come across the face there in the glass and was surprised to discover it stored backstage with the other discarded things.

Sofya Andreyevna came off the stage gasping.

"Christ, I need a drink!"

In a small fury now with the glass, the fury seeming the fiercer for its compactness in so small a person, Marietta Valentinova rubbed mightily. The glass squeaked under her hard fingers as if protesting the rubbing but revealed no more than the blurred image.

Christian knocked on the blackboard.

"You're on."

The stage was too small for the Czybulka that Marietta Valentinova had chosen—the *Rêve d'amour apres le bal*—but it was just as well she didn't have much ground to cover. She started to grow short of breath, and her knees began to hurt. The stove was roaring now, its sides turning red, from all the wood Mr. Farley had piled in it. People in the audience were shedding hats and coats, vests and sweaters. Marietta Valentinova's face glistened. The sweat ran down between her small breasts, and her hair was sticking to her face. By the time she took her bow and waited for Mr. Farley to close the curtain, she was exhausted.

"I am going to need some extra time," she said to the balalaika player.

She sat down heavily on the trunk. Her knees were swollen. As she massaged them, she thought, in a moment of panic, she would not be able to do her final dance, the Pavlova. She saw herself going onto the stage with everyone watching and her knees would not hold her, her breath would not last, and she would not be able to do it.

She shook her head to dislodge the thought. She knew that if she thought something bad, she could make bad happen. But the moment she succeeded in forcing out the thought, a new one entered. She tried to shake this one away also, but it did not go. And so she had to see herself again on a day in the spring, a false spring that was cold and gray and damp and her landlord had put a lock on Marietta Valentinova's thermostat so she would not use up the heating oil. She was doing her exercises at her bar by the window. As she looked out, she saw an old Russian woman in a black coat climbing the stairs of the hotel across the street. Halfway up, the woman had to stop. At the top she stopped again. Marietta Valentinova could see her shoulders rise and fall with a huge breath which at once the ballerina realized was not from the climb up those few porch stairs but to brace herself for the dark foyer of the hotel where the old woman lived and before long would die. Quite inexplicably, Marietta Valentinova found herself on her knees in tears.

Sofya Andreyevna peeked around the corner of the blackboard.

"Marietta Valentinova," she said smiling, her teeth red with lipstick.

The ballerina heard applause.

"Come and listen to this boy play the balalaika!" Sofya Andreyevna said.

The ballerina looked at her.

"Are you all right?"

Marietta Valentinova nodded.

The balalaika started up again. The notes danced the way a young girl might, swirling her skirts.

Marietta Valentinova eased herself onto her feet. From out of a plastic dry-cleaning bag she took her swan costume. Putting it on made her feel immediately better. It was of silk ordered specially from a store in Boston. The feathers she had obtained from a farmer on the Peavey Road who kept ducks. She touched the material of the skirt and tried not to think about her knees, or about any of the other, trying to think only of the next dance, the Pavlova. Finally she went to the curtain where Sofya Andreyevna and Mr. Farley were standing, he with the rope held eagerly in his big freckled hands, she with her arms folded atop her breasts, both watching the young man with the balalaika. He was out in the center of the stage, his hand in the fast part of the song a blur over the strings. For an instant after the song ended, the faces of the audience, full of wonder, seemed to float over the chairs, like a string of buoys carried by a wandering current into some quiet cove.

The applause was even louder than before.

Marietta Valentinova had to wait in the wing through three encores. Finally the young man got up and waved to the people, who were still clapping.

"You've got some nerve," she told him when he came off stage. "What do you think you're doing?"

"I thought you needed time."

"Don't get smart with me, young man. I am the professional here—remember that." Despite his gentle looks and quiet manner she could see he was a very conceited young man.

"I'm sorry."

"So you should be." She angrily waved him away. "Curtain," she said to Mr. Farley.

Her final dance was *The Dying Swan*. She told the audience that she was dedicating it to the memory of the great Pavlova, in whose company she once had had the pleasure of spending part of an afternoon in London.

The dance was all *pas de bourrée* and a few low arabesques.

Despite the pain in her knees, Marietta Valentinova felt she had never danced it better, never with more feeling. The feeling was the thing, she reminded herself; that was innate, not to be learned, not the way one learned to play a folk tune, for example, on a balalaika. Which was not to say that, if you were lucky enough to have certain inborn qualities, you did not have to work hard and, yes, suffer: suffer sometimes not only physical pain but other kinds like the indignity of having a lock put on your thermostat and waiting for people who did not know enough to show up on time and having to put up not only with the ignorance but impudence.

She could have done as others did, taken the easier road; gone to work at the poultry company, for instance, with good money every week and nothing to worry about—days off, health insurance, everything—instead of having to get by on the little money her parents had left her, devoting her life, her being, to the travail of her exercise bar. Day in, day out, *battement tendu, passant de gage, frappé,* stretch, kick: It wasn't easy.

You had to practice, of course, to play a balalaika, as you did any other instrument, but the music in a way was already in it, in the wood and strings and glue and the shape of the thing. You touched the right place, learned to strike the right string at just the right time, and the music came out but it was a part, really, not of the player but of the instrument, just as the beauty and passion and grace were *of* her, being innately in her, in her blood and bone. She was player and instrument both.

The early winter night was falling. Its darkness was at the windows now. The world had become small, come down to the hall with its stove and its people seated in the dark and above them the ballerina floating in the light as in a soft distant yellow sun. Marietta Valentinova was dancing effortlessly, as if for her the dance required no thought or effort at all. In the wing, Sofya Andreyevna smiled praise at her but the ballerina seemed as unaware of the old woman as she was of the people silently watching beyond the edge of the stage.

Suddenly Marietta Valentinova realized her knees no longer hurt. Her breathing was steady and strong. She wasn't even tired.

On an impulse she fluttered her arms and extemporaneously added some *entrechats* that, she felt, Pavlova's choreographer, Fokine, might well have put in if he'd thought of it.

After a few minutes the swan sank to the floor. Arching its long neck, it was about to die when the needle got stuck in the record. The music repeated on itself three or four times before the Reverend Mr. McFarland managed to poke the needle clear. Marietta Valentinova tried not to hear what she heard. On the stage the swan was dying with grace and great passion and beauty, and in the audience someone . . . laughed!

When she arose, her face was very pale. She stepped forward and took a stiff bow. She forced a smile as the Golikov girl brought to the stage the bouquet of roses that Marietta Valentinova had had delivered from the florist's. There was a polite round of applause as she accepted them.

They had only to see her face, that small face with its compacted ferocity. They watched her leave the stage, her face white in the places where it wasn't rouged, saw the face for just a moment as it retreated over stilt legs trying not to run, vanishing behind the blackboard. Quickly, without a word, they collected their things, their coats, their galoshes, and they got out, leaving the ballerina alone in the dim and the dust, WHY I LOVE GOD mounted over her head like some ancient motto over an iron door or tomb, the words faint but still discernible like something white standing in smoke.

For several minutes Marietta Valentinova, her lips pursed hard, her tiny fists knuckling, her breath whistling from her nose, swore terrible things at the three of them, the balalaika player, Sofya Andreyevna, Mr. Farley. They had better stay out of her sight! She cursed the baroness, the priest, and, for good measure, Tolstoy. She had begun to run through some others of those she had seen in the audience when she became aware of voices out in the hall.

She lifted her head and listened.

The people were still there. They were waiting for her!

Marietta Valentinova got out of her feathers and silk and into her street clothes as fast as she could. Wiping at the mirror with a tissue wet with tears and sweat, she repaired her face, touched her hair, brushed the shoulders of her dress. In the clouded glass she tried out a smile that would convey a sense of warmth but also a certain aloofness appropriate for a ballerina.

She pushed open the stage door. The audience was gathered at the front of the hall.

No one noticed her.

For a long time they did not go away. From the shadow of the doorway she listened to the baroness, imperious, self-centered, dictating as always, and she suffered the boyish, sanctimonious tone of the priest. At last the circle opened. From it emerged Christian with his balalaika. They were all around him: her guests, *her* audience. The young man came out and they followed him and when he paused at the stair to the outside door they gathered around him again.

At last they went away. Marietta Valentinova waited for the street outside to clear. She heard cars starting, voices calling good night. The hall lights had been turned off, the stove damped down. The cold was coming in, low over the floor. Gathering her gowns and phonograph, her records and her roses under her arms, Marietta Valentinova crossed the empty hall, a quick shadow in the moonlight.

At the top of the stair she stopped. Below her in the dark was a darker thing. She was a darker thing, too. In silence they stood like markers at the opposite ends of night. Then the thing below her moved a step forward.

"You done real good, Miss Valentine."

"You fool! You scared me half to death!"

Mr. Farley stepped back awkwardly.

"I just got to lock up this place."

"You shouldn't jump out at people like that," she said.

She brushed by him and went out the door. But outside on the snowy walk she stopped, her back to the doorway where he stood. "You said you liked it," she said over her shoulder, not looking at him.

He came forward eagerly then, as if exonerated. "It was awful good," he said.

"What about that boy? The one who played. I suppose you liked him, too?"

"He was good," said Mr. Farley. "But he weren't like you. Oh, no, missus—not by a long shot."

It was very cold, but Marietta Valentinova did not hurry home. Two or three times she paused to look up at the sky and inhale the air. The smoke from the chimneys stood over the houses like feathers in their caps. The moon and the stars shone down, lighting her path.

Most people were just awful, simply horrid, and not very

intelligent. Marietta Valentinova knew this very well, and accepted it. But now and then, she thought, looking up at the stars, one of them surprised you.

She had the idea that when she got home she would write a letter to Tolstoy's daughter. As far as she knew, the woman was still alive. She would let her know that although her father had set Russia on its ear, turned the whole world upside down, it was no reason for the Tolstoys to be smug. The countess might be surprised to learn that even in a godforsaken town, cut off from her rightful homeland, miles from anywhere, not even a movie house for a bit of entertainment, let alone a real theater or a nice restaurant, consequently some people losing the ability to distinguish between what was truly fine and what was not, for which you had to feel sorry for them—even then, there was one who was not going to let herself get depressed or be defeated, not by a Tolstoy, not by anyone.

And if the woman again didn't answer—well, that would say something about *her* intelligence.

Her gowns over her shoulder, Marietta Valentinova went along, following her shadow down the snowy street.

the
ice
fish

Maxim Maximovich was an educated man. He did not in
the least believe that Father Vladimir, the priest of the Holy
Virgin of Kazan, the church in the old ice house shed down
by the river, was a spy.

Maxim Maximovich and his wife lived with their daughter
Sonya on the entire top floor of the Hotel Nicholas the Second, the boarding house in which, on the lower two floors,
many of the town's older Russians also lived. The hotel had
once been the home of a sea captain whose schooner had

carried, to Florida and the West Indies, blocks of ice cut from the river at the foot of the hill. On the roof was a cupola and a widow's walk with an iron railing wrought with stars and eagles. On summer evenings Maxim Maximovich and the baroness liked to sit out there sipping cool drinks and gazing down upon the town and the river and the woods all around. Below them on quiet nights they could hear the chairs creaking on the veranda and they took pleasure in knowing that the old people, their fellow Russians, were out enjoying the same soft breeze, the very same sky filled with stars.

In their living room was a bookcase filled to the ceiling with books in Russian and English and some in French and German. In the bathroom was a rack of magazines that told about the stock market, movie stars, rich Arabs, and what the President and other famous people had done the previous week—so that whatever important was happening in the world, Maxim Maximovich was sure to know about it.

So when people like Sergei Andreyevich Palchinsky, the president of the local chapter of the Union of True Russians, said to him about Father Vladimir, "It's not just something people sucked out of their fingers," Maxim Maximovich might nod or shake his head and appear to agree that it was an awful thing. But of course he knew better.

To him, Father Vladimir was simply an old man, a little feeble-minded, a little set in his ways. But to imply or say outright, as did Mr. Palchinsky and many other members of Maxim Maximovich's church, the Church of Vasily the Blessed, that he was a Soviet agent . . . well, Maxim Maximovich had to laugh.

Mr. Palchinsky was the warden of Vasily the Blessed. Whereas Father Vladimir's church belonged to a branch of

Russian Orthodoxy that acknowledged the legitimacy of the patriarchate of Moscow, Vasily the Blessed belonged to the Holy Russian Church Outside of Russia, the church in exile. It didn't recognize the patriarch or anything else about the Soviet Union. Its members did not even like to say the words "Soviet Union."

As a young man, Mr. Palchinsky had fought in the Civil War against the Reds. One day in a battle a bullet had come along and clipped off the end of his nose. All he had left was a nub with nostrils that whistled slightly when he talked, so that he sounded as if he were accompanying himself on a little flute. This experience, of being shot in his nose, had left him with a terrible tremor. When he collected the offering in church on Sunday he sounded like a gypsy with a tambourine.

"He keeps a short-wave radio in his house—did you know that?" Mr. Palchinsky would say, putting his hands in his coat pockets, which then would flap like small wings. "A radio with a long antenna."

"I've never seen it."

"You don't think he's going to leave it out for you to see, do you?"

"What are you trying to say?"

"Do you know the kinds of places you can listen to with such a big antenna?"

"What kinds?" Maxim Maximovich would know exactly what was coming.

"Why ask? You know."

"No, I don't. Why don't you say it?"

"You don't need me to say it."

"Moscow, I suppose. Havana?"

"See? And you pretend not to know."

Then Mr. Palchinsky would remind him how Gregor Mironovich Smolnov, who worked in the kitchen of Maxim Maximovich's own hotel, had heard about a priest in a Displaced Persons camp after the war who was a *seksoty*—a Soviet informer. Was it just a coincidence that this priest, by all descriptions, should have a white beard and a bald head with a long fringe of white hair at the back of his scalp so that from the rear, it was said, he looked very much as he did from the front—just like Father Vladimir?

Maxim Maximovich knew the way the people thought. The more innocent a man appeared, the more they suspected he was up to something. To argue would have been like throwing peas against a stone wall.

One day early in Lent, Maxim Maximovich was in the bank for a closing on a chicken farm when he decided to pay a call on Father Vladimir. It was a cold gray day and people in the town were fasting. Maxim Maximovich watched them leaning grimly into the wind as they passed the bank window, their coat collars up, their chins tucked into their chests.

For some months he had been trying to talk the old priest into signing over his house and moving into the Nicholas the Second, where he would have every comfort. The house was little more than a shack—a tiny house with a tin roof and tar shingles fastened to the river bank like a nest to a tree. From the kitchen window you could look up and down the river and across to the pine woods, which lifted up the sun each morning and took the glow of its setting. That was when the idea had first struck Maxim Maximovich—at sunrise. He and the baroness had been on their way home from a party when the sun rose out of the woods and made a path of shimmering gold straight across the water to them. It had excited them very much.

Maxim Maximovich was not surprised that Father Vladimir at first did not appear eager to do it. People grow used to misery the way they do to wrinkles.

"I know you're only thinking of my own good," the priest had said. This was in November when the ground was freezing hard. "God bless you for it. You think I'm lonely, don't you?"

The next time, Maxim Maximovich had spent almost a whole afternoon in the priest's kitchen while the old man made sugar cookies. Maxim Maximovich told about all the other Russians in town who had entrusted their homes to him. As they grew older, it became hard for them to keep up with the taxes and all the repairs, especially in winter with the high cost of heating oil, not to mention the worry. Suppose your roof caved in under the snow? Suppose you got sick or slipped on the ice and hurt your back? How long might you lie there before someone found you? And even in spring your worries didn't end because the river might flood and your sump pump could break.

Now these people lived humming a tune in his wife's hotel. They were with people their own age; in the lobby they had card tables and comfortable chairs and even a color television set.

The old priest seemed to think about this. His mouth came out in a little spout and his white eyebrows knit together, as if his face were on a draw string.

Maxim Maximovich sat back confidently. He took a cookie from the dish Father Vladimir had set out and dunked it in his tea.

And that was the only thing the priest said anything about. As if Maxim Maximovich had not come with his briefcase and contract and his plan for a good life. As if he were some lady visiting from next door.

"My wife's recipe, God rest her soul," the priest said. "I'll give it to you if you'd like, Maxim Maximovich. Does your wife like to bake?"

At that point another real estate broker might have given up. But Maxim Maximovich knew better. All he had to do was wait. When the days grew colder and the world seemed to spin more slowly and it was dark more than it was light, a comfortable place where you could be was not so easy to turn your back on—no matter how old and stubborn you were.

As Maxim Maximovich sat in the bank, the radiator beside him gurgled with a happy sound, like a brook. His wallet, plump with his commission, pressed pleasantly against his heart. The owner of the chicken farm, a thin, nervous-acting American man with an oversized wife, shook his hand with such gratitude that Maxim Maximovich was afraid the buyer might change his mind. Except that the buyer, a Russian plumber from Brooklyn who had been mugged twice in the past year on his way to work, did exactly the same thing.

Maxim Maximovich emerged from the bank as onto a stage, stopping in the middle of the shoveled path and beaming up and down the street as if acknowledging applause on either side. His neck stretched as far as it would go, holding his head up high. With one foot in his car he paused again and for maybe a whole minute, like a hunter with his foot up on his trophy buck, smiled up at the gray cold sky as if it were full of sunshine.

Father Vladimir was kneeling at his morning prayers. When he heard the knock he turned his ear and listened.

Sometimes it happened that when someone knocked, no one was there.

Father Vladimir suspected a devil. Everything in the universe, whether it was a creature or a season or a feeling in your heart, had its opposite. Father Vladimir was pretty sure it had something to do with God deciding to make the world go around in a circle rather than in a square or triangular movement or just having it stand still. If God gave the world saints, He also gave it devils.

Yet Father Vladimir found it hard to abide them, even the ones who only played pranks. When he opened the door and one of them wasn't there, he was relieved but also very angry. You never knew where they were hiding or what they might do next.

He knew it was a sin to slam a door in anger. So when the knock came again, he said, "Dear me. I hope it's someone."

With whispered words that sounded like air being bled from a water pipe, Father Vladimir finished his prayer and crossed himself three times.

"Excuse me," he said. "I'd better see, just in case."

Holding up his skirts, he crossed the room to the door with watchful little steps, like a lady on a stair. The bottoms of his long winter underwear hung loosely around his thin ankles.

Instead of the devil off hiding somewhere, there in his doorway stood Maxim Maximovich, his face bright and shining like the moon.

Maxim Maximovich stamped the snow off his feet. He was smiling so broadly that you would think he was showing off a dance step that had taken a lot of practice to perfect.

"Maxim Maximovich! What a surprise! Do you know that only this morning I was thinking of you? Or was it yesterday? I said to myself, 'Well, I'm just going to have to have a talk with Maxim Maximovich.' I think it was this morning, but never mind. Come in, come in. How's your dear wife? I want to show you something."

"I can't stay long," Maxim Maximovich said. "How are you? It's an awful day—again."

"Thanks to your prayers, I'm fine."

"The discouraging thing is that the winter's not yet half-way through." Maxim Maximovich gave a shudder, although the house was warm. In a corner a wood stove was tinged with red. A pot of water was boiling on it, its rim wearing a hoary crust like an old man's beard.

Father Vladimir carried Maxim Maximovich's coat off to the closet with both arms. He gave a grunt as he hung it up, as if it were a side of beef he was hoisting onto a hook.

"They say we're in for another good storm," Maxim Maximovich said, rubbing his hands over the stove.

"Do you think so?" Father Vladimir said, emerging from the closet. "I love the snow. Just think, all those little flakes, every one perfect. To tell you the truth, I prefer the cold to the hot. I think it has something to do with Russian blood being thicker or thinner—whichever it is. In New Jersey where we lived you could hardly breathe in summer. Olga— God give her rest—would carry the electric fan with her from room to room, wherever she went. Have you been to New Jersey? We had a nice apartment there. But the heat in summer wasn't good for us. The air was so thick you could hang a hatchet on it. I sometimes wonder if it wasn't the fan blowing on her all the time that made Olga sick."

"All I can say," said Maxim Maximovich, "is that I'm very concerned about what this cold weather does to the heating bills of our senior citizens."

"It must be hard on them, poor things," Father Vladimir said sadly. "I wish I could do something, Maxim Maximovich."

"You know, when you're a child it's different. You think winter is wonderful. On my Sonya winter produces only red cheeks. But for old people . . . well, I don't have to tell you. Except it can be very tragic: You can get sick and even die."

"Maybe it would help," the priest said, "if I prayed for an early spring. I could start today."

"We all had better pray for something."

"That's an even better idea! Good for you, Maxim Maximovich! It may take a little time, but I'm sure God would go along if we all asked Him sincerely. Don't you think so?"

"But then the people should not be counting the days," Father Vladimir added thoughtfully. "You'll have to tell them that, Maxim Maximovich: Don't count. Tell them to imitate your daughter. Try to think of the ice and snow as a gift from heaven. When they see it's something wonderful they'll want it to last. But why are we standing here? You're not going already, are you? Why not stay and have a nice cup of tea? It seems like you've only just come."

Father Vladimir showed Maxim Maximovich to the kitchen table, then fell into a long silent conversation with himself, whispering in the way in which he prayed, as he fussed with the cups and spoons and paper napkins and the dish of cookies to put out. He had spent all his life studying the lives of the saints, pondering the gospels, and thinking about God and what it must be like in the Kingdom of Heaven. The few practical things he knew how to do were those he had learned from his late wife. While the slats dropped out of the shutters and the porch step wobbled and the chimney leaned over a bit more each year, on the inside the house was as tidy as a widow's room. The pans and cookie sheets over the stove gleamed like a wall of mirrors. The curtains smelled fresh from the wash. Every day he dusted the tops of everything, making a needle of the rag to get in all the tiny crevices in Olga's knickknacks. Once a week he scoured the toilet bowl and scrubbed the kitchen floor. He ironed not only his outer garments but his underwear and stockings. In the spring he picked violets in the grass out back and set them on the window sill in the sun.

"Now what was I thinking?" he said when the tea was ready and he had come and sat beside Maxim Maximovich. He thought a minute before remembering how just that morning or yesterday he had been looking out his window at the river and had started to think about something.

"Yes, it's depressing, isn't it?" said Maxim Maximovich. He gazed out the window. The world was bleak. The wind was blowing. Clouds of snow carried over the river as if the woods were on fire. Maxim Maximovich gave a sigh. How sad, he thought, that people preferred to patch up the reality of their lives with their thin little lies to themselves rather than to look at their true, threadbare condition.

If he had one attribute, he felt, it was his ability, his willingness and, yes, his courage, to turn pockets inside out, to shake the contents onto the table where things could be seen, once and for all, in plain view.

With his shiny round chin he pointed to the wood stove and said, "What do they charge for a cord nowadays?" and before the priest answered that it was ten dollars more than last year he already was nodding his head and saying, "It must be very hard on you."

"You'd better be careful with that chimney," he added. "It doesn't look safe to me. And you living all alone . . ." He clicked his tongue. "What kind of a life is that?"

"People come all the time, Maxim Maximovich. Oh, there's no end of those who want a chat now and then. Did I tell you who came to see me last week? Try to guess."

Maxim Maximovich frowned. "I know what you're doing," he said. "Don't you know what you're doing?"

Father Vladimir looked down at himself to see if he was doing something.

"You're trying to avoid the subject."

"No, I'm not, Maxim Maximovich." After a moment, he said, "So, how's your family?"

"The subject," said Maxim Maximovich determinedly, "is your condition—your *real* condition. What can the church be paying you?"

"Well, it varies."

"I don't want to go into it," Maxim Maximovich said. "I only ask to prove a point. The point being, it's not easy to get through a winter even if you do get paid regularly. I know you don't want to talk about this, but I'm going to make you. Sooner or later you have to face it."

Father Vladimir looked into his tea cup. "A priest doesn't need much," he murmured.

"I wouldn't worry," Maxim Maximovich said with a softened voice. ". . . if only you'd learn to look out for your own interest."

Maxim Maximovich then spoke very persuasively, he thought, about his plan for Father Vladimir, pointing out how the room and board could be deducted automatically by himself from the priest's Social Security check or other pension, so he would not even have to worry about that. Each resident of the hotel was entitled to two meals a day, breakfast and lunch. You could also have supper, but that was extra.

"There's always someone to talk to. You can play cards. You can sit on the porch and watch everything that goes on. You can reminisce. . . ."

"I don't like to do that, Maxim Maximovich. There's too much about the past that makes me sad. . . ."

"You don't have to do it," Maxim Maximovich hurried to say. "Only if you want to. Some people like to do it. It was only a suggestion."

". . . Russia, my poor mother—she had such a hard life. And my Olga . . . we never had any children, you know."

"You can watch television," Maxim Maximovich said. "Up on the hill we get Portland and Bangor both."

"Can you get *Little House on the Prairie?*" Father Vladimir asked.

"I don't know. I can find out. I'm pretty sure we can."

"How about *Fantasy Island?*"

"That, too," Maxim Maximovich said. "I'm almost positive."

Father Vladimir didn't say anything for a long while. Then he said, "Imagine that . . . Portland *and* Bangor."

The ladies and gentlemen of the Union of True Russians of Plankton, Maine, settled themselves onto the divan and into the soft chairs in the baroness's living room and the maid brought out the napoleon to go with their tea. The pastry was wonderful and creamy and they all took a second helping except for Mrs. Bukharin, who was fatter than some of the others and said she was on a diet. When they were done they set down their dishes and patted their napkins tidily in place on their laps and the arms of their chairs.

Mr. Palchinsky called the meeting to order. Mrs. Golitsyn, recording secretary, read the minutes. Mrs. Bukharin, the treasurer, gave the financial report. Then the baroness, who was their program chairman, introduced Father Alexey, who was going to speak on the return of Juan Carlos to the

Spanish throne, an event that had much excited the members. The baroness noted that Father Alexey had studied Spanish in college and had visited Mexico on vacation.

Father Alexey was sitting at the head of the tea table. He had a leg crossed as if he were relaxed, but you could see he was nervous. He was drumming on his knee with his fingers and looking around at the membership and nodding all the time as if his head were on a spring. From the wall a large portrait of the Tsar looked down with a patient expression, as if it too were waiting to hear what the priest had to say.

Father Alexey had the problem that he could not speak Russian too well, although he had studied it at the monastery and for a semester in college. And while he had picked up quite a bit since taking over the parish of Vasily the Blessed a year ago, the words he knew were mostly little words or church words or words with which to comfort people in the hospital. With big words, especially words about politics, he wasn't very good. When the baroness introduced him, he sat up straight, smoothed his long reddish beard between his moist palms, and said, "Man can only be glad, to have in Spain a king nowadays."

He hadn't got much beyond that when Maxim Maximovich came through the door in high spirits, as if he were on his way to a ball. He kissed his wife so loudly the ladies had to laugh. She scolded him jokingly to make them laugh more. That's why everyone liked them, they were just like regular people.

"Sorry, *batyushka*—sorry," Maxim Maximovich said to the priest and tiptoed to a chair. He was tall and plump and good-looking and though he was a very important man he still was like a boy, the ladies thought—always up to pranks to make them laugh. Sitting forward the way he was now with his chin on his finger tips he looked to them like a naughty angel. "I'll be good," he said and winked to Vera Zolotnikov.

Father Alexey resumed his speech. "In Spain," he said, "not like Russia." He hadn't any notes to read from, but he had rehearsed at home. "Example. Franco long time ago . . . he is saying he is not king, only working for meantime in king's house. . . ."

"In the palace," the baroness said to help out.

"He was regent," said Mr. Palchinsky, who knew.

". . . until he is old and dying," said Father Alexey. "After that is coming king."

"Juan Carlos," the ladies said together.

"Certain," said the priest.

Then one of the ladies said, "Do you think one could ever hope . . . ?" And they all seemed to sigh at once.

"Things not same," Father Alexey said. "But yes—maybe hope. Everybody's prayers to help, could be, could be, same is happening in Russia but I think no."

"But it's not inconceivable," the baroness said.

"Oh, wouldn't it be nice?" the lady who had asked said dreamily.

This idea led the company to speculate over who might become Tsar if the Communists got kicked out sometime soon: Grand Duke Vladimir, who was the Romanov pretender, or somebody else. The vote was in favor of somebody else after the baroness pointed out that the Grand Duke's mother-in-law by his second marriage was Jewish.

"Then it's impossible," the members agreed.

All this time, Maxim Maximovich was waiting. He couldn't repress his spirits any longer. "All done?" he asked when the priest's speech was over. "Then let's have a party!"

He took out his billfold filled with the money from the bank and showed it around the room, holding it the way you'd hold a bird, so you wouldn't hurt it.

"Here's the kind of day it's been for me," he said proudly.

Maxim Maximovich didn't say anything about Father Vladimir's house. But he let the company know that no sooner had he closed the deal in the bank than he had another desirable property ready to sign. At first glance the new listing might not seem much of a place but as people often told him, he said, he had an uncanny ability to "look into the water" and see what others could not.

When he looked at the old priest's house, as he had that first morning coming home from the party and as he had again today, looking back from his car as he drove away, he did not see just a little tin-roofed house. What he saw was the wide river and the rise of the land and the sun on the water in summer as the tourist boat steamed upriver from Bath. He saw the mooring you could have, and the restaurant and gift shop. Some of the hotel's residents were clever with their hands. They could make all sorts of embroidery and other Russian things that tourists would like to buy. And what was a house but boards and shingles? You could pull out the nails and pile the whole thing up in a day.

That was what a man with vision could see. But he did not say this, either.

When lunch was ready, the company moved into the dining room, where the maid, Lisaveta Stepanova, had set the long table with the dishes that her husband, Smolnov the dishwasher, had brought up from the hotel kitchen. There were potato and sauerkraut pastries, pickled mushrooms, beet salad, a tureen of hot borscht, eggplant caviar, stewed cucumbers. The baroness inspected to make certain there wasn't any meat or fish or sour cream. It was, after all, Lent. They had cheated a little with the napoleon. God surely could forgive them for that. But to cheat twice in a day—that was getting into real sin.

Smolnov didn't go but stood there smiling insolently as the guests entered. He was a cantankerous old man, and no one liked him. He had a shaven head and his ears and nose were purple. Before the DP camp and before the war he had been in one of Stalin's camps. People said that more than once he'd been so badly beaten he'd almost died. Frankly, Maxim Maximovich could see why. They kept him on only because of Lisaveta Stepanova, a sweet thing and a good worker—worth ten of him. Maxim Maximovich had him run across to the drug store for a box of chocolates, just to get him out of there.

Maxim Maximovich got the vodka from the refrigerator. They drank to the Tsar, to good luck, to themselves, and to the vodka before it got warm. Pretty soon they were all in a spirit to match Maxim Maximovich's.

Vera Zolotnikov sang a song. Mrs. Bukharin made a kerchief of her napkin and pretended to be a peasant girl. They traded the stories they loved to hear: how old Mrs. Florenskaya in her senility talked to her dead husband every day on the telephone; how Marietta Valentinova had hid backstage and wouldn't come out after the phonograph needle had got stuck during the grand finale of her winter ballet in the Methodist Church hall; how the Goncharov girl had run off with a Negro from the Coast Guard station, causing her mother to collapse with a stroke on the living room sofa.

But when they turned to what was new, their happy mood changed. The latest things, it seemed, were all about aches and pains and nursing homes and who was having trouble going to the toilet and who had come to town for whose funeral and whether during their time of bereavement they had spoken to people to whom they were not speaking. It wasn't so funny.

They were getting depressed. To change the subject, the baroness thought of a suspicious new thing about Father Vladimir. She had heard he bought a whole bag of nylon string the other day in the hardware store. Everyone agreed this certainly was suspicious but they could not think why it was till Mr. Palchinsky said, "A whole bag full? Don't worry—it's for something then."

"The Soviets again?" Maxim Maximovich said with a smile.

The club members shook their heads and looked angry.

"Even our string," one of them said.

"Little by little, stealing what they can."

In the afternoon, Sonya came home from school. By this time, the company was quite upset with the Communists. Mrs. Golitsyn was suggesting a special meeting to decide who the successor to the Tsar might be. This would show the Soviets that the Union of True Russians wasn't fooling around. At a look from her mother, Sonya dutifully shook each guest's hand, squirming her small fingers out the moment they were grasped, as if the larger hand were a trap that might hold her there. One or two of the ladies tried to make some small joke with her, asking had she any boyfriends in school. She ran to her room without an answer or even a smile.

It grew dark long before the time for night. The baroness lit candles. Maxim Maximovich rang downstairs for wine. Throughout the afternoon the heat generated by the circle of friends had condensed on the windowpanes; now it froze on the glass in exotic patterns. Not being able to see out into the street, yet knowing the cold winter was there, beyond the icy swirls and flowerlets, like a danger from which they were quite safe, made them feel as snug as if the candle flames glowing in the wine were warming fires.

It was now that the priest spoke. They watched the shadow and the light on his young face, and each of them was still.

"Don't make elephants out of flies," he told them. He was a little more tipsy than they had seen him at church suppers when there was vodka under the tables.

"These things about Father Vladimir," he said. "Remember, God does not scatter us over the earth like seeds and then forget about us. The earth is like a great garden. God gives us the sun, He gives us the water. And he gives us a third thing. How do you say it in Russian? The dirt from the cows and horses and chickens? You know—after it passes through? No, really," he said when the club members laughed.

"This is the thing that is like sin," he said. "The strange thing is, we need it also, as much as the other. But you have to be careful. If it gets too close, it burns—your flowers, your peppers, the things in your garden will die. But when it is not too close—and not too far—all right, it is good. Do you see the meaning?"

The company nodded tentatively.

"Too close . . . good-bye. But just the right distance . . . look how beautiful is the garden!"

The company was silent. It was a funny thing for a priest to say, even if he was young and a little drunk.

"It's certainly something to think about," said Maxim Maximovich.

"You can see that *batyushka* has put a lot of thought into it," the baroness told her guests.

"More wine, *batyushka?*"

Father Alexey took another glass and drank it down. He

turned to his hosts unsteadily and said, "Anyone who gives as much as you . . . I'm sure you must be tired."

"Never mind, tired," said the baroness. "Our people here are like our children. Sometimes I worry about them so much I get a headache."

"When you follow always a road that rises—well, you're bound to get tired," Maxim Maximovich said, coming to his wife's side. "That's what we keep telling ourselves, father."

Before the priest left, the baroness wrapped one each of the sauerkraut and potato pastries in a napkin.

"In case you get hungry," she said, and slipped it into his coat pocket.

The next morning when he awoke not feeling well at all, Maxim Maximovich raised the shade and looked into a winter fog. Suddenly it was warm: The flowers of ice had run down the windowpane and the roof was dripping. A little way off where the stores and houses hid in the fog, it was hard to know what was earth and what was air. Maxim Maximovich lowered the shade and went back to bed.

They ate breakfast in their bedclothes at noon. Lisaveta Stepanova, who was cleaning up from the night before, brought their juice and coffee and buttered toast. They divided the morning paper. Maxim Maximovich felt a little better. He said to his wife, "Pigeon, do we have anything we don't want? I'd like to give a little gift to Father Vladimir."

"Whatever for?" the baroness said, putting down her coffee cup.

"I don't know," he said. He had the back half of the paper and was reading the business news. "I feel sorry for him, I suppose."

"That's your trouble," she said. "You're always feeling sorry."

"It's the way I'm made, I guess," Maxim Maximovich said.

After a moment he peered over the top of his reading glasses.
"Don't we have some little thing?"

"I don't know, *dearest,*" she said, getting impatient with
him. "Look in the drawer. There's all sorts of junk."

"You pick something."

"Oh, really!"

"How should I know what to take?"

It was a bother, but eventually she found something. It
was an ikon of the Madonna of Czestochowa. It had been
given to them by someone who had not stopped to think
that Czestochowa was not Russian but Polish—and not only
Polish but Catholic.

"Are you sure?" Maxim Maximovich said. "It looks like
a nice one."

"What are we going to do with it? I'm certainly not going
to put it with *our* ikons."

"Well, it's up to you. I just thought it might be too nice."

Maxim Maximovich put it away in his briefcase. Then he
dressed and went down through the lobby. Some of the
residents, having eaten lunch, were asleep in the comfortable
chairs. Others were staring out into the fog. At the top of
the veranda stairs, Maxim Maximovich stopped. He thought
he heard a bird singing. It was a fragile sound; it seemed to
be far away but he could not be sure. As he went down to
his car the fog wrapped itself around him and he felt himself
unseen, a safe thing to feel. But as he turned by the river
and drove up the little rise to the priest's house the fog lifted.
All at once, there was the sky, there was the sun.

"Ah, Maxim Maximovich," the priest greeted him at the
door. "It's good to see you. And look, the sunshine! It's good
to see you both."

Maxim Maximovich opened his briefcase on the kitchen

table. He looked as if he were preparing to perform a magic trick. The first thing he took out was the ikon of the Madonna of Czestochowa.

"Forgive me if I embarrass you, Maxim Maximovich," the priest said. "But you're just too good." He took the ikon into the living room and placed it on the altar table in the corner where he prayed.

"We've kept it all these years," Maxim Maximovich said.

"Well, now you'll have a cup of tea," the priest said. "I've baked some of those sugar cookies you like."

"And the good news is, we get those programs," Maxim Maximovich said. "*The Little House on the Prairie* and the other one. I checked first thing when I got back yesterday."

"That *is* good news, Maxim Maximovich."

"I don't think they can get them everywhere."

"I'm sure they can't. They're just about my favorite programs. You really should try to watch them sometime, Maxim Maximovich. I'm sure you'd like them."

Maxim Maximovich took out the contract. He put on his glasses and looked it all over carefully, as if the words on it might have got juggled around in his briefcase.

"Here's what we were talking about yesterday," he said.

"Yesterday," Father Vladimir said. He brought the teacups to the table and he thought. "Of course!" he said. "I don't know where is my head. I forgot yesterday to show you." And he walked past the contract Maxim Maximovich was holding for him to see and he went into the shed. He returned with an armful of string.

"Nylon," he said, laying it on the table. He tested a strand with two sharp tugs to show how strong it was.

Maxim Maximovich started to read aloud from the paper he was holding.

"It's a net," said Father Vladimir. "Well, it's going to be a net. Maybe you can't tell yet."

"It's very nice," Maxim Maximovich said, trying to be patient.

"I think I can have it ready by spring. Guess what it's for."

"You tell me," Maxim Maximovich said.

"All right," the priest said. "But it's a bit of a story. Are you in a hurry?"

"Somewhat of a hurry, yes."

"Can you imagine, Maxim Maximovich, what it must be like to be a fish under the ice?" the priest said. "I was looking out of my window one day and that's what I was thinking. In summer it might not be so bad to be a fish—the water's warm and there's plenty of worms and bugs to eat. But how about in winter?"

"I can't imagine," Maxim Maximovich said dryly.

"Neither can I," said the priest. "But it must be awfully dark and cold down there. Three feet of ice and three feet of snow between you and the sky. They probably don't even know there's a sun in the heavens. They can't swim up, they can't look around. That would be the worst thing, I would think—not to be able to come up and see the world."

Maxim Maximovich looked at his watch.

"Anyhow, thinking about those poor fish reminded me about your real estate advertisements in the Russian newspaper," the priest said. "Do you remember the part about the sturgeon? Isn't it strange how these things come to you all at once?"

Maxim Maximovich squared himself in his chair.

"Father Vladimir . . ."

"I loved how you described things. You have a real talent, Maxim Maximovich. Come to Plankton, Maine, you said.

Snowy winters, cozy little houses, the green forest, a first-class hotel, sturgeon in the river, everything. . . . Just like Russia, you said."

The water was whistling in the kettle. Father Vladimir turned down the flame.

"Then I was looking out my window," he said. "And I thought, here's poor Maxim Maximovich worrying about how old people are going to survive—and out there sturgeon are swimming under our noses. Suppose we could catch one? Do you know how many roe are in one sturgeon, Maxim Maximovich? I don't either. I think there must be thousands, maybe a million. Just think if we could catch two! Do you know how much caviar that would make? I tell you, we've been living here with our arms folded."

Maxim Maximovich took off his glasses and said, "Let's be realistic."

"No one would have to worry then," the priest said. "I'm telling you, Maxim Maximovich. You wouldn't have to worry. The old people wouldn't have to worry. The town would be rich."

He took the string of the net in his hands and showed it, holding it out as if he were offering communion.

"We'll put it across the river," he said. "God gives us everything. Maybe he'll give us a sturgeon."

"Suppose there aren't any?"

"It said so in the newspaper, Maxim Maximovich. I can show you. Have you forgotten?"

"Suppose they went away?"

"Where would they go? They wouldn't go away."

"Well, suppose they did?"

"You should have more faith, Maxim Maximovich,"

the priest reproached him. "Just think of what it would be like, not having to live like a fish beating against the ice. Maxim Maximovich, we're going to have a real hope now!"

Father Vladimir watched Maxim Maximovich drive away. Steam was rising from the snowy street outside his window and from the roofs and trees of the town. It was as if suddenly underneath the snow, everywhere at once, there was warmth; as if all you had to do was push back the snow and there would be the earth, already in spring.

The priest smiled. He could still see Maxim Maximovich with the sun in his eyes, his foot down on the gas, scowling like a stepchild. He could hear what he would be saying to Sergei Palchinsky: "Well, you were right."

He had looked so comical marching out with his briefcase like a flag folded in defeat. Then all at once turning back to say it, the door usually being where you say what you had in your heart to say in the first place.

"Were you in a camp in Austria after the war? Just answer yes or no, if you don't mind."

And Father Vladimir had just smiled and said sweetly, "Three camps in all, Maxim Maximovich. Why do you ask?"

Father Vladimir closed the curtain and came back to the table. The kettle was softly whistling on the stove. People like Maxim Maximovich recovered quickly from their setbacks, he thought. In no time he would be himself again: thoughtful, judicious, refined. In that case he would not be saying anything so direct to Sergei Palchinsky. He was, after all, an educated man.

It would be something ambiguous.

"Father Vladimir an informer? Well, one never knows...."
Something like that. You didn't need much.

Father Vladimir put the net for the sturgeon away in the shed. Then he filled his teapot with the hot water and took a bite out of a cookie, smacking the sugar from his finger tips with little kisses.

prayer
for
the
dying

The day Yakov Kaputin died, he managed to make the nurse understand that he wanted to see Father Alexey. Yakov had lived in America for thirty years, but he did not speak English. He scribbled a faint wiggly number on the paper napkin on his lunch tray and pointed a long knobby finger back and forth between the napkin and his bony chest. "You want me to call, do you, dear?" the nurse asked in a loud voice that made Yakov's ears ring. Yakov could not understand what she said but he nodded, *"Da."*

When the telephone rang, Father Alexey was just dozing off. It was July. Crickets were chirring in the long dry grass outside his window. The priest was lying in his underwear listening to a record of Broadway show tunes on the new stereo set his mother had bought him. His long beard was spread out on his chest like a little blanket. The window shade was down and a fan was softly whirring.

He thought it was the alarm clock that rang and tried to turn it off.

"Mr. Kaputin wants you to come to the hospital," the nurse said.

He did not know how long he had slept. He felt shaky and unfocused.

"I can't," he said.

"Is this the Russian priest?"

"This is Father Alexey." His voice seemed to come from somewhere far away. "I'm busy just now."

"Well, we're all busy, dear." The nurse paused as if waiting for him to see the truth in that and do the right thing.

"What is it this time?" Father Alexey asked with a sigh.

The nurse began to converse chattily. "I just came from him. He's a real sweetheart. He wrote your number down. He didn't touch his lunch, or his breakfast. I don't think he feels well. Of course, we can't understand a word he says, and he can't understand us. . . ."

"He *never* feels well," Father Alexey said irritably. "You usually do not feel well when you have cancer."

"Well," the nurse said indignantly. "I've called. I've done *my* duty. If you don't want to come . . ."

Father Alexey sighed another large sigh into the receiver. He hated the hospital. He hated the way it smelled, the way grown men looked in johnny coats, the way Yakov's bones were all pointed. Besides, it was very hot out. During the entire morning service not a hint of a breeze had entered the church. In the middle of a prayer he thought he might faint. He had to go into the Holy of Holies and sit down.

"It's not a matter of 'not wanting,' " he said pointedly. "I'll have to adjust my schedule. That's not always easy to do. I don't know when I can be there. I have to try to find a ride."

He lay for a while longer with the fan blowing on him, his hands clasped on his soft white stomach. The sheet under him was clean and cool. He looked tragically at the window shade. It was lit up like a paper lantern.

Father Alexey lived next to the church in an old house with a cupola, fancy molding, and derelict little balconies. A rusty iron fence tottered around the unmowed yard. Once every seven or eight years one or two sides of the house got a coat of paint. The different shades of paint and the balusters missing from the little balconies gave the house a patched, toothless look. On rainy days water dripped down the wall next to Father Alexey's bed. He complained to Mr. Palchinsky, the president of the Union of True Russians, which owned the house. Mr. Palchinsky got the Union to provide each room with a plastic bucket. Father Alexey would have tried to fix the roof himself but he did not know how to do it. Yakov said he knew how to do it, but he was too old to climb a ladder and besides they did not have a ladder.

Yakov's room was next to Father Alexey's. Each night after the old man said his prayers he would say good night to the priest through the wall.

Father Alexey did not always answer. Yakov was a nice man, but he could be a bother. He was always telling stories about himself. Yakov in Galicia. Yakov in the Civil War.

Yakov in the labor camp. Yakov tending flower beds for some big shot in White Plains. Father Alexey knew them all. And whenever he made an observation with which Yakov did not agree, Yakov would say, "You're young yet. Wait a while. When you're older, you'll see things more clearly."

The priest knew it was one of the things people in town said about him: He was young. He tried to look older by wearing wire-rimmed glasses. He was balding, and that helped. Not that it was a bad thing to say, that he was young. If people really wanted to be disparaging—as when the Anikanov family got mad at him because he forgot to offer them the cross to kiss at their mother's memorial service—they went around reminding their neighbors that he was not Russian at all but an American from Teaneck, New Jersey; if they knew about his mother being Polish they called him a Pole; they brought up the fact that he once had been a Catholic. If they wanted truly to drag his name through the mud, they called him a liberal, even though he almost always voted Republican.

Yakov had been in the hospital before, once when he had his hernia and once for hemorrhoids. This time, even before they knew it was cancer, he sensed he wouldn't be coming home. He was, after all, almost ninety years old. He carefully packed his worn suit, the photographs of his wife, his Army medal, some old books that looked as if they had been rained on, into cardboard boxes, which he labeled and stacked in a corner of his room. He left an envelope with some money with Father Alexey and also his watering pail for his geraniums. When the car came to get him, he didn't want to go. Suddenly he was afraid. Father Alexey had to sit with him in his room, assuring him that it was all right, he was going to get well. He carried Yakov's suitcase out to the car. Yakov was shaking. When Father Alexey waved good-bye the old man started to cry.

The hospital was in the city, fifteen miles away. Once a week, on Thursday, the senior citizens' bus took people from the town to the shopping center, which was only a mile or so from the hospital, and you could get a ride if there was room. But if you did not have a car and it was not Thursday, you had to call Mikhail Krenko, the dissident. He had a little business on the side driving people to the city for their errands.

Krenko worked nights on the trucks that collected the flocks from the chicken barns. He had arrived in town one day after jumping off a Soviet trawler. It was said that he offered a traffic policeman two fresh codfish in exchange for political asylum. People suspected he was a spy. They were almost certain he had Jewish blood. Why else, they asked themselves, would the Soviets have given him up so easily? Why had he come to live in a godforsaken town that did not even have a shopping center?

Krenko was a small man with limp yellow hair and a round face like a girl's. He chewed gum to cover the smell of his liquor, sauntered with his hands in his pockets and did not remove his hat upon entering a house, even with an ikon staring him in the face. In the churchyard one Sunday, people overheard him call Mr. Palchinsky *"Papashka"*—"Pops." Anna Kirillovna Nikulin told of the time she rode to the city with him and he addressed her as Nikulina—not even *Mrs.* "Here you are, Nikulina," he said. "The drugstore."

Some female—an American; young, by the sound of her—answered when Father Alexey dialed his number.

"He's in the can," she said.

"Well, would you call him, please?" he said impatiently.

"Okay, okay. Don't have a kitten."

She yelled to Krenko. Father Alexey heard her say, "I don't know—some guy having a kitten."

When Krenko came on the telephone, the priest said as sarcastically as he could, "This is Father Alexey—the 'guy' from your church."

"Hey, you catch me hell of time, with pants down."

"I called you," Father Alexey replied stiffly, "because one of my parishioners happens to be very ill."

He hung his communion kit around his neck and went to wait for Krenko in the sparse shade of the elm tree in front of the house. Only a few branches of the old tree still had leaves. In some places big pieces of bark had come off. The wood underneath was as dry and white as bone.

Across the street from where the priest stood was the funeral home. Sprays of water from a sprinkler and a couple of hoses fell over the trim green grass and on the flowers along the walk. Father Alexey held his valise with his holy vestments in one hand and in the other his prayer book, a black ribbon marking the place with the prayers for the sick. He could feel the sweat running down his sides.

He thought what it would be like to strip off his long hot clothes and run under the spray, back and forth. He saw himself jumping over the flowers. He could feel the wet grass between his toes. Setting down his valise, he took off his hat and wiped his face and balding head with his handkerchief. He fluttered the handkerchief in the air. In a minute it was dry.

From behind him a window opened. He heard Mrs. Florenskaya call. He pretended not to hear her. He did not turn around until she had called for the third time.

"Oh, hello, Lidiya Andreyevna," he said, holding the bright sun behind his hand.

"Somewhere going, *batyushka*?" the old woman asked in her crackly voice.

"Yes," the priest said reluctantly.

"Good," Mrs. Florenskaya said. *"Ich komme."*

The Union of True Russians had bought the house along with the church building next door. It had been a fine, sturdy house, the home of a shipbuilder; the church had been the stable for his carriage horses. The Union divided the house into rooms and flats and rented them. At one time, they had all been occupied. Everyone was gone now, dead or moved away—mostly dead. The whole parish had grown older all at once, it seemed. Now with Yakov in the hospital, Father Alexey was alone in the old house with Mrs. Florenskaya. Every day she shuffled up and down the empty, echoing hallway in her slippers and Father Alexey would hear her crying. In nice weather she cried out on the porch. The first time he heard her—it was shortly after he had arrived to take over the parish, his predecessor, Father Dmitri, having been transferred back to New York after a prolonged bout with the bottle—Father Alexey had run upstairs to see what was wrong. Mrs. Florenskaya listened to his beginner's Russian with a happy expression on her face, as if he were trying to entertain her. Then she had replied in a mixture of English and German, although he did not know any German, that a bandit was stealing spoons from her drawer.

He no longer asked.

After a minute the front door opened and the little woman came spryly down the stairs carrying a cane she did not seem to need. A paper shopping bag and an old brown purse hung from one arm. She was wearing a kerchief and a winter coat.

"Where going *Sie*, little father?"

When he told her about Yakov, she sighed heavily. "Old people just closing eyes," she said. Her chin started to wobble.

"Aren't you hot in that coat, Lidiya Andreyevna?"

She pulled a wadded tissue out of her pocket. "*Sie* young man, *Sie* can *arbeiten*. I am old." She wiped her nose, then lifted her chin in the air. "I *arbeiten* in Chicago," she said proudly. "In fine hotel."

Father Alexey looked down the empty street.

"He's late," he said.

"*Ja*," the old woman said emphatically, as if he had confirmed all she had said. "Many *Zimmer* taken care of; wash, clean, making beds."

A short distance from where they stood the road dropped steeply to the river. Father Alexey could see the far bank and the dark pines of the forest beyond. The sky was blue and still. The leaves were motionless on the trees, as if they were resting in the heat. Above the brow of the hill, Father Alexey saw two heads appear then slowly rise like two plants pushing up into the sun. The heads were followed by two bodies, one long, one square. They came up over the hill and slowly in the heat toward the priest and Mrs. Florenskaya. They were dressed for the city, the woman in a dress with flowers, the man in a dark suit and tie. The woman was the long one. The man was hewn sheer and square like a block of stone. As they drew near, the man took the woman's arm in his thick hand and stopped her short of the shade. They looked back down the road. The man checked his watch.

Bending around the priest, Mrs. Florenskaya peered at them with curiosity.

"Good heavens," she said in Russian. "Why are you standing in the sun? Come here, dearies, with us."

The man gave them half a smile. "It's all right," he said as if embarrassed. But the woman came right over.

"Thank you," she said, as if the shade belonged to them. "That hill! We had to stop four times. Stepanka, come join these nice people." She pulled him by the arm. "Now that's much better—no?"

Father Alexey introduced himself and said in Russian that the weather was very hot.

"Fedorenko," the man said but he did not offer his hand. He added in English: "My wife."

"Ach, Sie sprechen Englisch!" Mrs. Florenskaya said delightedly. "I, too!"

From time to time Father Alexey had run into them in the market or on the street. The man was Ukrainian, the woman Byelorussian. The woman would always smile. Occasionally the man nodded stiffly. On Sundays Father Alexey would see them pass by on their way to the Ukrainian church.

"Are you waiting for someone?" the man's wife asked, continuing the English. "We're supposed to meet Mr. Krenko here."

"He was supposed to be here ten minutes ago," the priest said.

"We're going to do a little shopping," the woman informed them. "Stepan's not allowed to drive. It's his eyes. They wouldn't renew his license. We're going to get some glasses for him. He doesn't want them. He thinks they'll make him look old."

"Not old," her husband said sharply. "Don't need it. What for spend money when don't need it?"

"You see?" she said hopelessly.

As they waited the sun grew hotter. They inched closer together under the tree. They could see the heat coming up from the road and from the shingles of the roofs that showed above the hill. Mrs. Fedorenko fanned her face. Mrs. Florenskaya unbuttoned her coat. They stared longingly at the shimmering spray of water across the way. There was a rainbow in the spray and the water glistened on the green grass and flowers and lawn sign on which the undertaker had painted in gold an Orthodox cross beside the regular Christian one.

Finally they heard an engine straining. Up over the hill through the waves of heat came Krenko's car. It was a big car, several years old, all fenders and chrome. Upon reaching level ground it seemed to sigh. It came up to them panting.

Krenko pushed open the front door.

"You're late," Father Alexey told him. With a look of distaste, he set his valise with his holy vestments on the zebra-skin seat cover. Mr. and Mrs. Fedorenko climbed into the back, followed by Mrs. Florenskaya, who nudged Mr. Fedorenko into the middle with her bony hip.

"Where is she going?" Krenko said.

"Ask her," the priest shrugged.

"Where you going, lady?"

"Never mind," Mrs. Florenskaya said.

"Not free, you know. Cost you money."

"*Ja.* Everything all time is money."

"Ten dollars," Krenko said.

"*Ja, ja.*"

"You have?"

Mrs. Florenskaya took a rag of a bill out of her pocketbook and waved it angrily under Krenko's nose. She put it back and snapped her purse. "Everything is money," she said. Tears suddenly rolled out from under her eyeglasses.

"Crazy old woman," Krenko muttered.

"May we go?" Father Alexey said.

They drove around the block onto the main street of the town. On the street was the market, the bank, the hardware store, the laundromat, the Hotel Nicholas the Second, and the variety store. Part way down the hill Krenko stopped and blew the horn.

"Another passenger, I presume?" Father Alexey said.

"Make it when sun is shining," Krenko said.

From a door marked PRIVATE stepped Marietta Valentinova, the famous ballerina who lived over the hardware store. A white cap with a green plastic visor kept the sun from her small severe face. Krenko got out and opened the front door, giving her a mock bow, which she ignored.

"Good afternoon, Marietta Valentinova," Father Alexey said. *"Ya yedu v gospital."*

The ballerina glanced at his valise. One corner of her small red mouth lifted. "The hospital? Well, I thought you have been looking thin," she teased him in English. "That's the trouble with being monk: no wife to feed you."

"It's Yakov Osipovich," he said, reddening.

"So," she said. "Shall you move over or must I stand in sun all day?"

"Maybe you get in first, lady," Krenko said. "With such little legs you fit better in middle."

"I will thank you to pay attention to your own legs. And also to your manner. Who do you think you are, blowing that horn?"

"Like joking with her," Krenko winked when the priest got out to let the ballerina in.

"How about the air conditioning?" Father Alexey said when Krenko got back behind the wheel.

"Okay. First got to put up all windows," Krenko said. He

turned a switch. Air blew out from under the dashboard.

"I think that's the heat," said Father Alexey.

"Is okay," Krenko said. "Got to cool up."

They drove to the bottom of the hill and turned up along the river. The water lay flat and colorless between banks of colorless clay. Soon they were in the woods. The road ran over the tops of the hills and down to stream beds filled with rocks. The undergrowth was dense and tangled and they could no longer see the river. They passed a farmhouse with a barn propped up by poles. In a clearing slashed in the woods a mobile home squatted like a gypsy, its children and its trash strewn around the yard.

The air was blowing out of the vent, but the car was stifling. They were squeezed together, Father Alexey with his valise on his lap. Marietta Valentinova smelled Krenko's sweat. She moved a fraction closer to the priest, who had pulled out his handkerchief and was wiping his face.

"If I don't get some air, I am going to faint," Marietta Valentinova said.

Krenko clicked the switch another notch. The hot air blew out harder.

"Sometimes takes couple minutes," he said.

"In a couple of minutes we will be cooked," the ballerina said. "Can't you see I'm dying?"

"Hold it!" Krenko said. He felt under the dashboard. "Now is coming."

Father Alexey wiggled his fingers in the air blowing on his knees. It was still hot.

"*Now* is coming," Krenko said confidently.

"Open a window," the ballerina commanded.

"You going to let all the air condition out. . . ."

"Did you hear me?" she said in a voice so severe that everyone at once rolled down the windows.

"Thank God," said the priest as the wind blew in on them. They put their hands out into it, groping for a current of coolness.

After a while, Mrs. Fedorenko said, "It was very hot in New Jersey, too. That's where we lived."

"Hot like hell," Krenko agreed, although he had never been to New Jersey. "Here is not hot."

"I am very glad to hear that this is not hot," the ballerina said. She held a hanky over her mouth as they passed a chicken barn.

"More hot in California," Mr. Fedorenko said. "I been all over United States. Many Ukrainian people live in California. Many Russian, too," he added for the benefit of the ballerina, who had cocked her ear toward him, showing him her profile, the raised eyebrow. "And many Ukrainian. Not same thing."

"Do tell us about it," the ballerina said haughtily. To Marietta Valentinova there was no such thing as a Ukrainian. That was modern nationalistic nonsense. What was the Ukraine?—*Malorossiya*, "Little Russia." They were all Russians.

"You are from New Jersey, *batyushka*?" Mrs. Fedorenko asked to change the subject.

"Yes. It is very hot in New Jersey. I haven't been to California."

"*I* in Chicago *arbeiten*," Mrs. Florenskaya said.

"You were saying something about the *malorossy*, I believe?" the ballerina said.

"Not Little Russians, lady. Ukrainian."

"All right, Stepanka. Did you hear? *Batyushka* also lived in New Jersey."

Mr. Fedorenko folded his heavy arms. "Don't call us *malorossy*."

"I don't call you anything," the ballerina smiled coldly.

"No?" Mr. Fedorenko pushed forward his big chin. "What are you calling ten million Ukrainians? The ones Russia starved?"

"If you are speaking of the Soviet Union, I'll thank you not to call it Russia," the ballerina said. "I hate that word—*soviet.*"

"Okay," Krenko said. "Long time ago—okay?"

"I have a question," Father Alexey said.

"You, too," said Mr. Fedorenko accusingly. His face was very red.

"Me, too? What?" said the priest.

"Stepanka," Mrs. Fedorenko implored.

"I see you Four July parade. See you turn away when Ukrainian club marching by. You don't remember, huh?"

"I didn't turn away."

"I wouldn't blame you if you did," the ballerina said. "I certainly would."

"I didn't."

"That's enough, Stepanka."

"Maybe I just looked somewhere else," the priest said. "There is a big difference between looking somewhere else at a given moment and turning away."

"Of course there is," Mrs. Fedorenko assured him.

"I know how is seeing," her husband said.

"All right, Stepanka. What were you going to ask before, *batyushka*? You said you had a question."

"I don't know," the priest said dejectedly. After a moment he said, "I guess I was going to ask why everyone is speaking English."

"You're absolutely right," Mrs. Fedorenko said. "You need to practice." And then she said something in Russian, or

Ukrainian, or Byelorussian, which Father Alexey did not quite catch. In the conversation that followed, he heard many words he knew but there were many words in between—they spoke so quickly—which he could not understand.

Then there was silence.

He looked around and saw the others were looking at him.

"*Nu?*" the ballerina said.

"*Shto?*" he asked. "What?"

"*Shto ty dumayesh?*"

"*Shto?*"

"Heavens, my dear Father Alexey," the ballerina changed to English. "We are talking about poor Mr. Kaputin. Haven't you been listening?"

"Of course I've been listening."

"Well, then?"

"Well, what?"

"Does he have much pain? Is he getting any weaker? You did say you were going to see him? He's not going to last, is he?"

"Yes, of course, Marietta Valentinova. I know. I understand." He had picked out Yakov's name in the wash of words that flowed back and forth between them, but he had heard the word, he thought, for "flowers," and he assumed they were talking about the old man's geraniums. Yakov grew them in his window box. They were big, healthy flowers, all from pinchings from other people's flower pots, and it was the thing you saw when you walked past the house. Instead, they had been discussing his funeral. Father Alexey shifted the valise on his lap. His clothes were stuck to him.

"The nurse said he wasn't feeling well," he said. "Who knows what that means? The last time they said the same thing and I went all the way to the hospital and there was nothing wrong with him. He was fine. He just wanted some-one to talk to. I walk in and he says, 'I'm glad you came, *batyushka*. Have you paid my electric bill? I think I paid it before I came here, but I can't remember.' I told him every-thing was taken care of. 'That's good,' he says. 'I was wor-ried. So how are you, *batyushka*? It's hot out, isn't it?' That cost the church ten dollars."

"Don't blame me," Krenko said. "They don't give the gas away."

There were more farms, more rocky fields, and unpainted houses that tilted one way or the other. Then more woods broken by raw-cut clearings full of stumps and weeds and plastic toys and house trailers on cement blocks.

Of the farms and houses, Father Alexey could almost pick which were Russian, which American. None of the people in them had money, you could see that easily enough, but the American ones almost seemed to be the way they were out of stubbornness. There was something willful, in a sav-age, defiant way, about the broken porches, the rusty ma-chinery outside the barns. The Russian yards were unkempt only with weeds and overgrown grass and the woods coming closer and closer. They had little gardens, just tiny patches, with flowers and a few vegetables. Father Alexey started to get depressed.

"Did you ever think," he said, looking out the window, "that you would be here?"

No one said anything.

"Are you speaking to me?" Marietta Valentinova said.

"Yes. To anyone."

"Who would ever think they would be here?"

"Then why did you come?"

"Personally, I came for my health."

Mr. Fedorenko gave a guffaw. His wife pulled at his sleeve. "It's true. Why else would I leave New Jersey? I had a nice place to live in. When I danced I got good write-ups. You should see the people who came to my ballets. You could barely find a seat. The only thing was, the air was no good to breathe. All that pollution. If you dance, you must have air. So where does a Russian go? You've got to have a church. So you go where there are Russians. At least in New Jersey there were people with intelligence," she added over her shoulder toward Mr. Fedorenko.

"So many people lived in New Jersey!" Mrs. Fedorenko said before her husband could say anything. "We like it here, though," she added, patting Mr. Fedorenko's thick square hand. "We've had enough big things—the war, DP camps. After the last camp we went to South America. On Monday morning you turned on the radio and if there was a revolution you did not have to go to work. Too many things. Here it is small and quiet. Stepan always wanted to live next to a river. He says that with a river you will never starve."

"I live in this place eighteen year," declared Mrs. Florenskaya. *"Achtzehn Jahr,"* she added for Father Alexey's benefit. "All in this old house."

"Eighteen years," said the ballerina sadly. "I couldn't stand this place so long." But she already had been in the town more than half that.

Father Alexey calculated. Eighteen years ago he was nine years old. It was a whole year in his life, but all he could remember of it was being in the fourth grade and Sister Rita St. Agnes being his teacher, a stern woman with thick black eyebrows who had seemed to take to him after his father died. "The boy with the laughing eyes," she had called him affectionately. Sometimes he'd looked into the mirror to see why she'd called him that. The eyes belonged now to a not very old person who was expected to be full of answers for people far older than he, people who were afraid of getting sick and of nursing homes and hospitals and of what was going to happen to them. He dispensed answers like the holy water he flung on heads and shoulders at feast-day processions. Answers for death and fear and sadness and stolen spoons. And in all his life he had only lived in New Jersey with his mother and in the monastery in New York and now in a little town no one had ever heard of. How could he know?

In another eighteen years he would be forty-five. How much would he know then? Would he see things more clearly, as Yakov said? Krenko and the ballerina might still be around. Krenko probably would be in jail or involved in some scheme, making money one way or another. The ballerina would be an old woman if she were still alive. The others would surely be dead. Most of the people in the parish would be dead.

He was becoming more and more alone in the world.

The shopping center was on a broad avenue that ran between the interstate highway and the city. Once the road had had fine old houses with wide porches and broad lawns and beds of marigolds and tulips. A few of these houses remained, but now dentists and lawyers had their offices in them. The rest had been torn down for the fast-food restaurants, gas stations, and bargain stores that lined the road with their bright, colorful signs like a crowd at a parade. Krenko drove into the shopping center parking lot and discharged his passengers in front of the K-Mart store. He would be back for them in about two hours, he said.

Father Alexey let the ballerina out and got back in the front seat. His cassock was wet and wrinkled where the valise had been.

"Look like you piss yourself," Krenko laughed.

In the hospital Father Alexey carried his valise in front of him to hide the wet place. Two teenaged girls snickered behind him on the elevator. A small boy who got on with his mother gawked up at him all the way to the seventh floor. "Hey, mister—you look like something," the boy said.

Father Alexey marched to the nurses' station and set his valise down impatiently. Then he remembered the wet place and covered it with his prayer book.

"You're here for Mr. Kaputin?" asked the nurse who was there.

"Yes," Father Alexey said curtly. "Are you the one who called?"

"No, that was Mrs. Dinsmore. She's gone off shift now." The nurse came out into the corridor. She was a tall woman with narrow shoulders and graying hair. Even before she said anything, Father Alexey knew from the look on her tired face that Yakov was going to die.

"The doctor has been in," she said.

He followed her to the room. Yakov was asleep, long and gaunt under the sheet. There was a sweet thick smell in the room. Yakov's bones looked as if they might pop through his face. With each breath his mouth puffed out like a frog's throat. On the stand beside his bed was the ikon from his bureau at home and a small vase of daisies whose petals were dropping off.

Father Alexey touched the old man's arm.

Yakov's eyes blinked open. For a while he stared up at the priest.

"It's you," he said.

"How are you feeling, Yakov Osipovich?" Father Alexey asked in Russian.

"I saw my mother." Yakov's voice was hoarse and very old. He took a long time between his words.

"Where did you see her?"

"She went away. There are fewer Russians, *batyushka*. . . ."

He began to talk incoherently, something about apples in his father's orchard. The words came out in pieces that did not fit together, as if something inside of him had broken.

The nurse brought a glass of tea. Father Alexey cooled it with his breath.

"Here, Yakov Osipovich," he said, raising the old man's head. The tea rose halfway up the glass straw, then sank back into the glass.

"Try again, Yakov Osipovich. Pull harder."

"Shall I try?" the nurse asked.

Father Alexey took his communion kit from around his neck. "I don't think it matters," he said.

The nurse went out quietly, leaving the door ajar.

Father Alexey arranged articles from his kit and others from his valise on the stand beside Yakov's bed. He put on his holy vestments. He took the ribbon from the place he had marked in his book, and turned through the pages to the prayers for the dying.

He read quietly, occasionally making the sign of a cross over the old man's head. Yakov gazed up at him in silence and a kind of wonder, his mouth agape.

The priest softened a piece of bread in a little wine.

"Yakov Osipovich," he said. "Are you sorry for your sins?"

The old man looked from the priest's face to the hand with

the bread. Then his eyes closed. Father Alexey shook him. "Yakov Osipovich," he said. "Say, yes."

He tried to put the bread into Yakov's mouth but the old man's teeth were clenched. He slipped the bread between Yakov's lips, tucking it back into his cheek. Eventually Yakov's mouth began to move. He chewed fast, as if he were hungry.

Yakov opened his eyes just once more. Father Alexey was putting his things away. He heard Yakov's voice behind him. The old man was looking at him calmly.

"How did you come?" he said.

The priest sat down beside him. "I found a ride. Are you feeling better?"

"Then you have to pay."

"Don't worry about it, Yakov Osipovich."

"Well, I'll straighten it out with you later, *batyushka*."

Krenko was parked outside the emergency door in a place marked DOCTORS ONLY.

"You make me wait long time," Krenko said. Father Alexey could smell liquor on him.

"I'm sorry."

"Not me, I don't care. But little dancing lady going to be mad like hell."

Marietta Valentinova sputtered at them half the way home. Tiny drops of saliva flew from her mouth and landed on the dashboard. Father Alexey watched them evaporate, leaving little dots. At last she stopped. They became aware of his silence.

"*Batyushka?*" Mrs. Fedorenko said.

After a while Krenko said, "Well, you got to go everybody sometimes."

"Where going?" Mrs. Florenskaya said.

"Mr. Kaputin," Mrs. Fedorenko told her gently.

"*Ja, alles,*" the old woman said. "*Alles kaput. Mein Mann, meine Kinder. Alles* but me."

The sun was gone from the window shade when Father Alexey got back to his room and lay down on his bed. It was still light, it would be light for a while yet. He turned on his fan to move the air and looked at the wall through which Yakov had said good night. He heard Mrs. Florenskaya in the hallway upstairs. She was starting in again.

The priest switched on the stereo set with the record from the afternoon. But still he could hear her.

"Christ," he said, and turned up the volume very loud.

(1985)

the girl
who
would
be
russian

Mrs. Brown's daughter was one hundred and ten pounds overweight and still living at home in her room upstairs when she decided at the age of thirty-one to become a Russian.

Her transformation began the night she'd gone to the hotel and heard the Russian band playing its songs. Mrs. Brown didn't become aware of it till the following week when the girl brought home the bellyliker and shut herself in her room with it, hot as it was that summer. It made a noise that was not like any music Mrs. Brown had ever heard.

The next thing Mrs. Brown knew, her daughter, whose name was Debbie, was calling herself Natasha and going around saying *Na zdorovie* and *Kristos voskres* to everybody. Because these words—which meant, Mrs. Brown learned later, "Here's to you" and "Christ has risen"—did not carry Debbie very far in conversations, she filled in with English that sounded Russian.

"Be so good, pliss, as to passing salt," she would say to her mother at the dinner table. "Tank you."

Mrs. Brown's first suspicion was that Debbie, like her father, had secretly taken up drinking, which had killed him in the end. She searched Debbie's drawers and closet and looked behind the chimney plate, which was where Wallace used to hide his, but was unable to find the bottle.

After dinner each evening and on the weekends after lunch and sometimes after breakfast the girl would disappear into her room. Thereafter from behind her door would come a furious striking of strings. From time to time Mrs. Brown would be startled by a yip and a wild cry of *"Na zdorovie!"* Looking up from her ironing or from her *Good Housekeeping* magazine, she would let out a big sigh.

These were the times when Mrs. Brown thought of Wallace. What would he say, she wondered, if he knew that his only child, who was qualified by her ancestry to join up with the Daughters of the American Revolution, was behaving like one of the foreigners in town?

Mrs. Brown remembered when the first Russian family moved into Plankton twenty years ago. They bought the Potter place, Francis Potter having moved to Connecticut with his family to look for work. People would drive by on a Sunday afternoon to get a look at "the Russian house." The family's name was one you couldn't pronounce, *Vish-*

something. The first thing they did was dig up Francis's front yard and put in potatoes and the second thing was to build a chicken coop out back. Mrs. Brown supposed that if you were still allowed to keep pigs in town, they would have had one of those, too. Wallace, who was forever making excuses for people, including himself, said he did not see any particular harm in spading up the Potters' nice lawn or having a few laying hens out back or, for that matter, a few Russians in town.

The trouble was, they didn't remain a few. Pretty soon up came everybody else—uncles and cousins and sisters and nephews and people who had lived in the same village in Russia as the *Vish*-somethings or had been in the same camp after the war or who had known them in South America where they went first.

Then all of this crowd brought up *their* relatives. It wasn't long before you could not go into the store without bumping into a whole bunch of them talking Russian just as loud and bold as you pleased even though they were in this country now and ought to be made to speak English, Mrs. Brown thought, by law.

"We let you into this country," Mrs. Brown told one of them in the middle of town one day after the man had taken the parking space she had wanted, "and this is how you treat us!" She said it right out, not caring who heard her.

And what did the man do but fold his arms on his chest and laugh at her *in defiance!*

The trouble with Wallace and that whole family of his, Mrs. Brown thought as she rocked herself on the swing-couch on the piazza, rocking faster the madder she got, was that right through the generations they had about as much practical sense as a snake had hips. All you had to do was to look at the land that once had been theirs. At one time they had owned clear down to the river. And they had let it all slip through their fingers, some pieces lost to squatters and others in card games until there was nothing left but the farm and not half a living to be made from it for a widow with a grown daughter who was growing stouter every year and turning into an old maid even faster than she was turning into a Russian.

Mrs. Brown's frown deepened so that her mouth nearly touched her chin.

"It would be just like that man not to open his mouth to her," she decided of Wallace.

It was July and between the earth and the sun there was not a breeze or a cloud. In the field across the road the hired men were bringing in the last of the day's hay. Mrs. Brown was paying them by the hour. She watched irritably as they tossed the bales onto the wagon, moving as if work were a painful act that you had to ease yourself through as slowly as possible.

"If there's one thing I can't stand," Mrs. Brown said out loud in a reproachful voice, as if Wallace were somewhere nearby trying to keep out of sight, "it's weak-willed people who are afraid to say boo, even if it's for a girl's own good."

She put down her magazine and walked resolutely to the screen door. She called up the stairs to Debbie. For an answer she got a thwang of bellyliker strings.

The next morning at breakfast, Mrs. Brown said in a very pleasant voice, the way she had always believed a mother and her daughter should converse, "Deborah, I've thought of something nice for us to do this weekend."

She could not see Debbie's face behind the newspaper but

she heard the impatient way her daughter blew out the smoke from her cigarette.

"Please put the newspaper down, dear," Mrs. Brown said. "I want to talk to you."

The girl lowered the newspaper just enough to blow a stream of smoke that barely missed her mother's head. "Go ahead," she said indifferently.

"I wish you wouldn't smoke at the table, Deborah."

"Anything else?" Debbie said.

All that was visible of the girl were her plump fingers and her braids, which were pinned up the way some of the Russian women wore their hair in the *National Geographic* she'd found in the stack in the attic. The braids made her ears look big but at least it was better, Mrs. Brown thought, than the way she looked when she'd come home from college, her hair hanging down her face like one of those protesters you saw on television who smoked marijuana and did not want to defend their country in Vietnam.

Mrs. Brown sighed loudly and deeply and regretfully enough she would think for a daughter to hear and put down a newspaper, but the girl went right on reading. Mrs. Brown thought sadly how once she had been such a sweet child although she had always been overweight and not pretty at all, having taken after Wallace's side of the family, and even now, at her age, tending to get pimples, which Mrs. Brown attributed to the fact that she did not have a boyfriend, which could make a girl break out. She did not help her appearance with her constant cigarette, which she let dangle from the corner of her mouth, her left eye squinted up in the smoke. To see her, anyone would think she'd grown up in one of those mobile homes with all the trash strewn around them instead of in a nice clean home for which any normal girl would be thankful.

After there was no reaction whatever to a second sigh of such force that it sent the smoke wafting back over Debbie's braids, Mrs. Brown said, "What I want to talk to you about is, I thought it would be nice this weekend if we could go over to the Waters' place for a visit. Vernon's back home," she added in a softened tone, trying to put a little melody into her voice. "I saw his mother in town yesterday. She said to come on over. You haven't seen Vernon for a long time."

"*Kristos,*" Debbie muttered.

"I don't know what that means, Debbie," Mrs. Brown said reprovingly. "I only hope you are not taking the name of the Lord Our God in vain."

Debbie clapped her paper shut.

"Clara Waters says that Vernon is pretty soon going to be one of the higher-ups at that label company," Mrs. Brown continued in a pleasant-sounding voice. "She says they make labels for a lot of your name-brand clothes."

"Hooray," said Debbie, "for Vernon Waters."

"I've always thought he was a nice boy," Mrs. Brown said. "And he hasn't got a stomach, the way so many young men have nowadays. Too bad," she added thoughtfully, "that men have to get stomachs."

"I've got to get going," Debbie said. She dragged on her cigarette, then doused it in her coffee cup.

Mrs. Brown did not know where she had learned such things. She looked distastefully at the butt in the saucer. "I thought maybe we could run out in the afternoon so it wouldn't look as though we expected dinner," she said.

Debbie was digging in her purse for her car keys. "Why not?" she shrugged.

"Why not what?" Mrs. Brown asked.

"Why not go? Why not dinner?"

Mrs. Brown's face lifted from its dropped position. "I'll call Clara right away," she said.

"As long as we don't stay late," Debbie said. Then she added in her English that sounded like Russian, "Saturday night vee playink balalaika."

The Andreyev Russian Classical and Folk Music Orchestra of Plankton, Maine, played each Saturday night in the dining room of the Hotel Nicholas the Second. The hotel stood on the main street at the top of the hill, above the bank and the laundromat and the hardware store. It had once been the home of a sea captain. For several years the Women's Christian Temperance Union had its Home for Little Wanderers there. The current owners, Maxim Maximovich and his wife, the baroness, called it a hotel, but it was in fact a boarding home for Russians in town who had become too old to keep up a house of their own. The hotel's dining room was the only place in town to eat, if you did not count the variety store, where you also could buy beer and pizza to go, and on Saturday night a few local people would go there for dinner and some Russians would come out of their rooms and listen to the music if they felt all right.

It was in the hotel that Debbie had first heard the balalaika. Someone at the bank where she worked had told her about the band, and one night she went. The band consisted of four old men and the leader's twelve-year-old granddaughter, who banged the tambourine not so much to enliven the music as to cover the orchestra's mistakes during difficult passages.

Debbie ordered vodka and quickly got a little drunk. During a break in the performance she got talking to Nick, the leader. He said he owned an extra balalaika he could let her have for three hundred dollars. There was a crack in it but Nick said it could be fixed with a little glue. The next week when Debbie went to the hotel, Nick had the balalaika waiting for her. She took it home and filled the crack with Elmer's Glue. After practicing every day until she could find five chords, she went back to the hotel with the balalaika and Nick even let her sit in with them for a number.

Now every Saturday night Debbie sat at the table next to the band and when the music started she pulled out her balalaika and fingered her five chords. The band allowed her to do this on condition that she not touch the strings, for she did not know which chords went with which music. Nick did, however, permit her occasionally to yip, which she had learned to do rather well. Debbie's one hand fluttered in the air over the strings like a large white moth dancing around the porch light while the other raced up and down the neck pressing what seemed to be the notes of the song and unless you were sitting right in front of her at a time when the tambourine was not being banged, you could not tell that she was not making any noise.

One time an old man who lived upstairs even came up and congratulated her on her playing.

"You are Russian?" he asked.

"Hahf," Debbie replied. She laid her hand on her large breast. "Thees hahf," she said, "where iss my heart."

Some nights Debbie showed up in a gypsy costume, weighted with beads and bracelets and earrings as big as baseballs. Other nights she came in an apron, skirt, and blouse she'd embroidered with designs similar to those she saw in the *National Geographic*. She came in a yellow Russian *sarafan* and in a purple gown with a tiara that sparkled with purple sequins from the K-Mart store in the shopping center in Augusta.

One night when the men were turning their music to the next number, Debbie said, "Just a minute, Nick. I think a bit of an introduction is needed here." And she went out in front of the band and in a dreamy voice said, "Next iss song about vooman dreaming of pahst lover. In Roshia, vee are calling song, *Tsiganka*. In English you are saying, I tink, 'Jeepsy Girl.' "

After that she introduced numbers whenever she chose. She also introduced the members of the band at the beginning of the evening and after each break when they came back to their places.

"And I," she would say, not forgetting to include herself, "am Natasha," even though almost everyone knew she was Mrs. Brown's daughter, Debbie.

The thing that Debbie liked most about being a Russian was that there weren't so many of them. When she was in college it had been fun for her to wear her hair long and march in campus protests without a bra and make older people feel indignant, but there was also the feeling, she remembered, of going back to the dorm having had fun yelling and chanting with kids your age and that night seeing the demonstration on television and trying to find herself in the crowd and then starting to feel funny, partly sick and partly sorry, as if she had been caught in an act of theft or betrayal, realizing that she could not find herself because no one in that whole bay of faces looked any different than anyone else.

Russians, at least, looked like something. She liked the way they could talk to each other in the store and no one else could understand. It was like knowing a password or secret handshake. Debbie couldn't imagine using such a language to convey anything mundane or trivial. When Russians talked, she was convinced, they talked about nothing less than Life itself. She was sure they all had suffered tremendously. To suffer could not be much fun, Debbie felt, but if you had, it made you a lot more worldly and added immeasurably to your value as a person.

The only bad thing about being a Russian was knowing it wasn't going to last forever or even for very long. Most of the Russians were very old. Some of them were of such an age they could say they had met Tolstoy in person or had been given a medal by the Tsar or once had been at the Villa Rodye listening to the gypsies when Rasputin staggered in drunk. Almost every week there was a funeral.

Debbie could see the day coming when she would be the only Russian left in town.

Debbie was in her room getting dressed. She had decided to go to the Waters' as Natasha. She put on her wide skirt with the petticoat that showed and the blouse she had embroidered with flowers to match the plastic ones on the wire head band that she slipped over her braids. As she sat on the bed pulling on her red boots, she knew exactly what her mother was going to say. But she didn't care.

Mrs. Brown was out on the front lawn when Debbie appeared on the porch. Mrs. Brown took one look at her and said, "You're *not* going like that." Debbie had been watching her mother through the screen door. She was picking pansies. The garters of her girdle showed as she bent over. Debbie could hear her humming to herself. For a moment she had felt sorry for her, she looked so happy.

"Don't start, Mother."

Mrs. Brown's burdened shoulders rose and fell heavily.

"Look, would you rather I stayed home?" Debbie said. "Because I'd be happy to."

"I don't know why you take such delight in doing this to your mother," Mrs. Brown said. "If this is the way you want to act . . . I'm sure Vernon will be very impressed."

"Screw Vernon."

"That's nice talk from a young lady."

In the car Debbie smoked two cigarettes, one right after the other. Mrs. Brown drove the whole way with her face angled toward the window. They didn't speak until they reached the Waters' driveway.

"Please, for your father's sake if not for mine," Mrs. Brown said. "Try to act like an American."

"And how, pray tell, is that?"

"I'm warning you, Deborah."

"I'm warning you, Mother."

Mrs. Brown pulled a tissue out of her sleeve.

"Oh, for God sakes," Debbie said.

"There's Clara, out on the porch," Mrs. Brown said. "Wouldn't you know it? And now you've got me all upset."

Mrs. Brown parked the car by the barn and blew her nose. She waved the tissue weakly at Mrs. Waters.

"Hay fever, Constance?" Mrs. Waters said as they came up. She looked Debbie up and down. "My," she said, "aren't you the pretty one."

"Tank you," Debbie said.

"Vernon! Look who's out here!" Mrs. Waters called inside. "Vernon's watching television," she said.

"I know I won't recognize that boy," Mrs. Brown said. "All grown up and a real businessman. He loves his mother, too," she added for Debbie's benefit. "That's a real son for you."

"He takes after his father," Mrs. Waters said. She called inside again. "In more ways than one."

They went up onto the porch and Mrs. Brown held out her bunch of pansies.

"Why, you're just as sweet as your daughter is pretty," Mrs. Waters said. "Debbie here looks like a bouquet all by herself. Ain't them boots awful hot?"

"Not at all," Debbie said. "We wear boots a lot."

"Well, you just sit a spell. I'll put these in water and get you something nice and cool to drink."

Mrs. Brown sat on the wicker settee. Debbie sat on the rocking chair and rocked.

"Keep your legs together, Deborah," Mrs. Brown whispered.

"My, isn't it nice out here?" Mrs. Brown said when Mrs. Waters returned with a pitcher of lemonade and four tall glasses. "A nice little breeze, too. I was just telling Deborah, Clara, how nice it is on your porch."

"Vernon'll be out as soon as the inning's over," Mrs. Waters said. "Debbie, I don't guess you've seen Vernon since high school."

"Isn't it a shame?" Mrs. Brown said. "That entire class has just vanished. I guess Deborah and Vernon are about the only ones left—and both still single."

Debbie began to rock harder.

"Never mind, Debbie, you two are the smart ones," Mrs. Waters said.

"My, yes," Mrs. Brown said. "I've always said to Deborah, 'Now you don't be in a hurry; you just take all the time you want deciding.' "

"No fear about Vernon hurrying," Mrs. Waters said. "When

it comes to girls, that boy's slower than the second coming of Christ."

"Of course, Vernon's away, too," Mrs. Brown said. "But not so far as everybody else—like when our Deborah here was in California that time."

"Young people have to go their own way, Constance," Mrs. Waters said.

"Deborah was out there in college," Mrs. Brown said. "She's got her degree."

"Here we go," Debbie muttered.

"Vernon might have gone to college if his father hadn't died," Mrs. Waters said. "He left us in a real pickle, that man did. At least Wallace had the sense to have insurance."

"Wallace was a wonderful provider," Mrs. Brown said warmly.

"Vernon's done all right without college," Mrs. Waters said. "I ain't saying he couldn't have done better, but he's done all right."

"You've got every right to be proud of him, Clara," Mrs. Brown said reassuringly. "I was telling Deborah how Vernon's almost one of the higher-ups over at Harrison Label now. Bet you're happy to have him home, though."

"He's got his own office since last week," Mrs. Waters said. "He's been all over on business, too—Bangor, Portland, even down to Boston."

"You hear that, Deborah?" Mrs. Brown said. "Even down to Boston!"

"Imagine," Debbie said.

"I don't like traveling much," Mrs. Brown said. "Wallace was selling spare parts when we first got married. Took me up to Aroostook County. I said, 'My, look at all them potato fields.' "

"My sister Ethel has a nice place in Fort Fairfield," Mrs. Waters said. "They got a big potato farm."

"I bought a bag of Maine potatoes last year that was all rotten on the insides," Mrs. Brown said.

Deborah made a snort as if she was blowing out smoke. "Is Vernon inside?" she asked. "I can't listen to this anymore."

"Why, we're just having a nice conversation," Mrs. Brown said.

"He's in his father's study," Mrs. Waters said. "Through and to your left. That's where we got the second TV," she said to Mrs. Brown.

As she went inside, Debbie heard her mother say, "Have you noticed, Clara, how young people just aren't good at making conversations anymore?"

The shades were pulled down and the study was dark except for the glow from the television and in the dark, like twin apparitions, the white soles of Vernon's bare feet on the arm of the couch. Debbie stopped in the doorway. Vernon lay slab-still except for his eyes, which he shifted to look at her for a moment, like a man sighting up a target, between the V of his feet. His gaze drifted back to the ball game. "What kind of an outfit you call that?" he said.

Debbie looked down at him on the couch. She did not answer right away; she did not want him to think his question was worth an answer. "This, Vernon," she said finally with a large degree of disdain, "is what one wears when one plays in a balalaika orchestra, as I do. I do not expect you, however, to know what a balalaika is."

She came into the room, strolling between Vernon and his ball game. She leaned back against the desk opposite

him, spread out her skirt with the petticoat that showed and
waited for Vernon to say something, but he didn't.

"And may I ahsk," she said after a while, "who is veening?"

"Veening?" said Vernon. "What's that?"

Debbie laughed, as if amused by her mistake. "I forgot,"
she said. "You don't speak Russian, of course. *Veening*," she
explained, "is a Russian term which, when used in the con-
text of a sporting event, means the team that is making the
most runs."

One end of Vernon's mouth pulled itself up into a smirk.
"Well, if that's what it is, it ain't the Red Sox that's doin'
it."

Debbie looked from one end of Vernon to the other. He
still had his knobby knees and his not very good teeth but
his hair was still blond and wavy the way Debbie remembered it from high school. His stomach peeking from under
his T-shirt looked as fresh and tender as bread in a pan.

"Vacation, Vernon?"

"If that's what you want to call it," Vernon said without
looking at her. "Next time, I ain't stickin' around here. Maybe
I'll go to Boston. I been there sometimes."

"That's very worldly of you, Vernon."

"I been there lots of times. They got this whole section
they call the Combat Zone. You can't imagine the things
they got there."

Debbie was trying not to look at Vernon's stomach. The
hairs on it were soft and yellow like the hair on his head.

"Vernon, I'm wondering that if in a house like this there
is something stronger to drink than lemonade?" she said.

For the first time since he had sighted her up between his
feet, Vernon looked at her.

"How much stronger?" he asked.

"A whole lot stronger, I think, Vernon."

When Vernon stood he was much taller than Debbie had thought he would be. He went around her to the back of his father's desk and took out a bottle of whiskey.

"Now you're talking," Debbie said.

Mrs. Brown could not see that her daughter was a little drunk when she came out onto the porch later with Vernon.

"Here's our two kids now," Mrs. Brown said boastfully. "I bet you didn't recognize her, Vernon, did you? I don't think you have ever seen our Deborah before in the full bloom of her womanhood."

"It's in the car," Debbie said. Vernon followed her down the porch steps in his bare feet. They went over to the car, Vernon jouncing on the gravel in the driveway. Debbie opened the back door and got out the balalaika.

"That's the thing that she plays," Mrs. Brown said, watching them from the porch. "It's a bellyliker."

"What's it do?" Mrs. Waters asked.

"Makes a racket," Mrs. Brown said. "But somehow those Russian people seem to like it."

"Figures," Mrs. Waters said. "It wouldn't surprise me if one day we got a bunch of them Veetmanese in town as well."

"That would be the next thing," Mrs. Brown agreed. She was looking out at Debbie and Vernon. "They seem to get along nice, don't they?"

Mrs. Waters squinted to see the distance to the car. "Well, at least he ain't mopin'," she said. "Been spendin' his whole vacation in front of that television set, mopin'."

"Seems to me, a young man like that needs someone nice," Mrs. Brown observed.

Vernon came back to the house. "Gotta get my shoes," he said. "We're goin' to town."

"You just make sure you're back in time for supper," Mrs. Waters said when Vernon came out with his shoes on. "Mrs. Brown and Debbie are going to be eating with us tonight."

"That's too much trouble for you, Clara," Mrs. Brown said. "Heavens, we're not looking to be fed."

"I got a nice roastin' chicken," Mrs. Waters said. "You hear me, Vernon? What's that you got in your pocket?"

"Nothin'," Vernon said and thundered down the porch stairs.

The two women watched their children walk together down the driveway. Mrs. Brown thought they looked like the rain barrel and the drainpipe but she wouldn't have said that for the world. There was something innocent and hopeful and sad in the way Debbie walked swinging her balalaika, like a little girl on the way to school with her books; it made Mrs. Brown's heart ache.

At the fence Debbie turned. "I'm going to show Vernon where we play," she called. *"Na zdorovie!"* The fat jiggled on her bare arm as she waved.

"She speaks a real good Russian," Mrs. Brown said to Mrs. Waters.

The heads of the cows in the pasture followed Vernon and Debbie as they walked in the heat under the cloudless sky, his shoes and her red boots already powdered with the roadside dust. Debbie played her five chords for Vernon and sang a bit of the song, as far as she could recall it and imitate the words, about the gypsy dreaming of her lover.

She sang it a little, then stopped and said, "Okay, Vernon, when I get to that part you've got to yell, *'Ga-ree, Ga-ree!'* "

"How come?" Vernon said.

"Because that's how the song goes, Vernon. Now let me hear you say it. 'Ga-ree, Ga-ree!' "

"Ga-ree, Ga-ree," Vernon said spiritlessly.

"Right. When I get to that part. I sing it, then you yell it out, *'Ga-ree, Ga-ree!'* That's how they do it in the band."

"Ga-ree, Ga-ree," Vernon repeated. "What's it mean?"

"It's a song about a gypsy," Debbie said. "It's probably her name."

"Ga-ree, Ga-ree?" Vernon said indignantly. "What kind of a name is that?"

"Her name's just *Ga-ree*, Vernon. Only you say it twice. Like, Vernon, Vernon."

"That don't make sense," Vernon said.

"Look, Vernon, it's only a song. When I reach that part, I'll point to you and then you yell it—okay?"

The first time Vernon missed his cue but after that he did it right and as they came onto the road to town Debbie was singing the song and Vernon was saying the words in the right place and they smelled the hay in the fields and saw the birds chasing in and out of the corn. The road ran straight between the farmsteads. In the distance they could see the cupola on the Hotel Nicholas the Second and the dome and the cross of the Church of Vasily the Blessed. Debbie had never been out walking in her Russian outfit before and pretty soon she started to sweat. Her blouse stuck to her and got wet and so did her petticoat that showed and she tried to pull it from between her legs while she walked along playing the balalaika for Vernon. When they came to the cemetery, Vernon said, "Why don't we go in there and sit for a while under those trees? You look like a sheep that just got dipped."

They sat on a knoll in the old part where the trees were tall and the grass was cool in the shade. The older headstones were worn thin from two hundred years of rain and snow and none stood straight; they leaned forward and backward at the same perilous angle, as if they had been positioned that way not by frost and the heaving of the earth but by sculptors or poets or maybe priests who meant them to be symbols of the moment of falling. The mounds before some of them bore faded little flags like the sheenless flowers of autumn and on the stones were the names of men and the regiments of old wars, and there were tiny stones for babies and stones for young women who probably had died in childbirth, birthing the babies who were there beside them, and some stones were altogether white, with the names and dates washed away so you couldn't read them.

Leaning against a tree they looked up through the high branches at the blue sky and lolled their heads against the shaggy bark and felt the earth damp and cool beneath them even in the summer day that had made them sweat. Down the hill, across the path that bore in from the road, the cemetery spread out in the hot sun toward the schoolyard. Out in the open near the fence were the graves of the Russians.

Vernon took the bottle of whiskey from his back pocket. "Look at them crosses," he said with indignation. "How come they got all them cross pieces going across instead of just one like every other religion?"

He took a swallow of the whiskey. He wiped off the mouth of the bottle and passed it to Debbie.

She matched his swallow and said, "Those are Russian crosses, Vernon. Don't tell me you've never been to the Russian church?"

"I don't go to church," Vernon said with stubbornness in his voice. "If I did, it'd be an American one."

"Well, if you ever chose not to limit yourself, you might

find out that when a Russian goes to church he just doesn't cross himself once, he crosses himself three times, sometimes more. Like this." Debbie crossed herself three times to show him. "That's how come their crosses are like that."

"Well, that don't make them better than anybody else," Vernon said.

"Who says they are?"

"Everybody who comes to this town anymore wants to see where the Russians live. They ain't no better than anybody."

"At least they've been somewhere, Vernon. How many people in this town can say that?"

"I been somewheres."

"You, Vernon. But how about other people?"

"My grandfolks when they got married went to Portsmouth, New Hampshire, on their honeymoon. Even way back then people been somewheres."

"Being in New Hampshire isn't being somewhere, Vernon. It's just like being here."

"Well, Boston ain't like here. They got things there'd knock your eye out."

"I'm talking about places like Moscow, Vernon. Shanghai. Buenos Aires. That's what I mean by somewhere. Nick's been to all those places."

Debbie saw Vernon look at her. She raised the bottle to her lips. "Just a man I know," she said.

Vernon watched the whiskey make a ripple on her smooth throat as it rode down, soft like a wave on the water.

"I never knew a girl before who could drink straight from the bottle and not even make a face."

"It's only whiskey, Vernon. We're used to vodka. It's a lot stronger."

"I don't like vodka," Vernon said. He leaned back on his elbows. "I guess I just like sex."

Debbie looked at him. He had moved his gaze out over the graveyard. He was staring keenly ahead, nodding a little, as if the thing he was talking about, the sex, was out in the sun by the fence and he was taking its measure.

"I just got a very high sex drive," he said, not looking at her. "Lots of women have told me that. I just got to have it all the time." He got the bottle back and took a fast swallow, a big one.

"Me, too," Debbie said, staring straight ahead now, also. She felt her heart start to pound. "I just can't live without it."

The bottle went back and forth between them. They tried to control their breathing. Debbie felt herself fast losing an advantage of words and wit and intellect, as if the beating of her heart were drumming it away. "I think it's really good," she said, swallowing hard to get it out, "to be able to say these things to each other. Because most people can't. It's so hard to find someone you can relate to about things that concern us all as human beings."

"Yeah," Vernon said.

As they lay there not looking at each other, as if the looking might require some knowing of what to do next, a line of cars came up from the town with their headlights on. The first car was the hearse from Payson's, the funeral home. It pulled into the cemetery and the others followed, like the tail of a snake. They drove in through the gates and then from the main path went down one of the side paths into the new part of the cemetery that was out in the sun. They stopped at a place where a grave was open and there was a pile of flowers and a pile of dirt.

A man in black whom they recognized as Mr. Payson, a tall man with a long blank face that somehow remained expressionless even when he laughed, got out and opened up the back of the hearse; then other men in dark suits stood in two lines on either side of the door and took out the casket and carried it to the grave. Father Alexey, the priest from Vasily the Blessed, climbed with difficulty out of one of the cars. Adjusting his long black garment, he walked with his smoking censer to the graveside, taking up position near the pile of dirt.

"Russians," Vernon whispered.

For no reason that they knew, they ducked behind the tree. Debbie reached stealthily around and got her balalaika. Vernon pulled in the bottle of whiskey.

Debbie looked out and said, "There's Nick down there." Then they looked at each other and started to laugh. In mid-laugh, Vernon leaned over and kissed Debbie on the mouth. In all of her thirty-one years, such a thing had never happened to her, and she liked it pretty well. But then Vernon was digging his bony knees into her and his lips that were soft at first became like two pieces of wire. Debbie opened her eyes. She saw a face fused to her own and a huge eye, like that of a monster god.

She tried to wriggle free. "Okay, Vernon," she said out of the corner of her mouth as it was being kissed.

Vernon didn't stop. He dug in harder with his elbows and knees and his hurting mouth that was now like wire. Debbie got her hands under his shoulders. "Vernon," she said, warning him. She shoved as hard as she could. Then she heard it break.

"Oh, no!" she said.

Vernon, who had not been prepared to be shoved, bounced

back on top of her joyfully, as if he had been tossed from a trampoline in a stunt, and being thrown was what made it fun.

Debbie squirmed to get out from under him. But now he had ahold of her.

Her hand found the whiskey bottle.

"You let me up, Vernon, or you're going to get it."

Vernon grabbed her by the wrist. She clawed at him with the other hand and he grabbed that wrist, too, and pinned her to the ground. She yelled and screamed and tried to buck him off.

"You broke my balalaika!" she cried.

He might have put a hand over her mouth to keep her still but he didn't dare let go because she had the whiskey bottle. He tried using his mouth instead. She bit him on the lip.

Vernon sat up quick. "Why'd you do that?" he said. "Now you got me bleeding."

"Good! I'm glad!" Debbie said. "This is your last chance, Vernon. Get up or I'm going to really scream."

"Go ahead."

When she did he told her once to stop. When she didn't, he didn't know what to do. He tried giving her a hard butt in the face with his head.

Immediately, she stopped screaming. She looked up at him in amazement.

"There," he said uncertainly. "I told you to stop, didn't I?"

Debbie's face turned red. The expression on it seemed to clamp down, like the visor on a suit of armor.

"All right, Vernon—now you're really going to get it!" she said.

She struggled mightily. She bit at Vernon's arms. She kneed him in the groin. She tried to get him in the face with her spit.

At last she began to cry.

"You're a bastard, Vernon."

He shook her wrist. "Come on, let go of that bottle. Then we'll go to town and you can show me where you play like you were gonna."

"First you're going to get killed!" Debbie said and she struggled some more but soon she was exhausted. She opened her hand. Vernon kicked the bottle away.

"Give in?"

Debbie turned her face away.

"Say that you give in and I'll let you up," Vernon pleaded. He squeezed her wrists hard. "Say it!"

"I give in," Debbie said.

"That's better," Vernon said. He sat back on her. "Okay, I'm gonna let you up. But don't try anything. You promise not to try anything?"

Debbie's eyes were shut hard. Her mouth was puckered tight, as if she were going to try spitting again.

"Say it," Vernon said.

"I promise," Debbie said at last.

Vernon let her up. Debbie picked up her balalaika. Its face was caved in. Vernon was kneeling in the grass feeling his bitten lip. Debbie held the balalaika on her lap as if it, not Vernon, was the one in pain.

"It ain't busted that bad," Vernon said. "I bet I know somebody that can fix it."

Holding the balalaika as if it were a baby, she slowly rose and started to walk away.

"Wait a minute," Vernon said. "Ain't we going to town?"

"I'm not going anywhere with you," Debbie said. She had the ruined balalaika in her arms, her cheek against its neck as if to soothe it.

Vernon followed her for a few steps. "How about a guitar?" he said. "I know this fellow's got this guitar he wants to sell. I betcha you could buy it real cheap."

Debbie turned around furiously. Her face was all bunched up.

"You're stupid, Vernon. You're a stupid, ignorant American and I hate you!"

Vernon watched her go down the hill. Her skirt was wrinkled in back and stained with grass and right in the middle it was stuck between her buttocks.

"Ha!" he cried. "Go on to your damned Russians! You're the one that's ignorant!"

The grave was not so far away that the mourners, suffering in the sun in their hot funeral clothes, could not hear the noise from the hill—not only hear the shouting but the laughter as well and then the sound of anger and then the sound of tears. Affronted, they glared up the hill—but they were afraid. Even before they saw the woman come out from the trees in her red boots and soiled skirt and the flowers askew in her hair, a braid fallen over her ear, they hurried to get away because they knew that among Americans were many who were dangerous and very often mad.

Someone among them—it may have been the countess who lived on the Plunketts' old farm—shouted, "Leave us alone!" as the woman approached with her bruised and swollen red face. Nick, who was among them, looked at Debbie, at the broken balalaika she held in her arms like a baby.

"Are you crazy?" he said.

Debbie tried to smile.

"*Kristos voskres*," she said timidly, as if it were an Easter service and not a funeral upon which she was intruding, as if she expected someone to reply, "Yes, truly, He has risen."

Father Alexey, who had thrown in the first shovel of dirt, hurriedly made the sign of the cross over the grave.

"This grave is sealed until the general judgment and the future resurrection," he said.

Then all the Russians got in their cars and, locking the doors, drove past the mad American woman and out the gate.

sarajevo

It did not take long after confession Saturday night for half the Russians in Plankton to know what Mrs. Shostakovich had done twice. The other half either did not own telephones or they did not answer them in the evening when some good television programs were on. A lot of Russian people in town liked to start out Saturday night with *Lawrence Welk*, who played the kind of music that did not hurt their ears, and stay up right through *Love Boat*, knowing that there would be plenty of time during church services Sunday morning to catch up on whatever local news they may have missed.

It wasn't a matter of eavesdropping—as those who had been in church could attest. Mrs. Shostakovich's words seemed to hang in the cold air, like the snow in a glass paperweight with a miniature winter scene. Everything, one witness said later, seemed to stop: the prayers, the conversations among the people waiting to confess, even the wind that rattled the windowpanes.

Looking up from his place before the ikonostasis, Father Alexey stared out over the congregation as if the silence were a presence, as if a stranger suddenly had entered the church.

"Go on, Sofia Mikhailovna," he said softly, putting a finger to his lips so that Mrs. Shostakovich might lower her voice.

"It's worse than you think!" she cried.

The people looked at each other in wonder. Some made an effort to resume their prayers to God and His saints but it was hard for them to concentrate. Everyone seemed to tilt forward. One of the ladies had the presence of mind to step out and quiet the men who were having a smoke in the vestibule.

Father Alexey managed a smile. "I'm sure it can't be that bad, Sofia Mikhailovna. Have you broken your Lenten fast?"

"Worse than that!" said Mrs. Shostakovich, her face wrinkled up with woe.

"They gave you too much change at the store," the priest guessed. "And you forgot to return it—we've all done that from time to time."

"God have mercy on me!" Mrs. Shostakovich said at the top of her voice. "I'm an adulteress!"

"I beg your pardon?" said Father Alexey.

"Two times!" Mrs. Shostakovich cried.

The shocked congregation remembered that on her way out, Mrs. Shostakovich had her shoulders hunched up as if to hide the shame burning on her face. The people said she did not look at all forgiven.

As for Mr. Shostakovich, the husband, he knew what his wife had done once, since he had been for his part responsible; but of the twice he did not know. It was the kind of a thing which, if you knew it, you would not say to a husband in his face. Smolnov the pot scrubber, who was Mr. Shostakovich's best friend, was the kind of a person who might have said it to him in his face if he knew it, but Smolnov did not go to church even for the holy days, let alone for vespers and confession, and people usually did not like to share news with him because he was also the kind of a man who, instead of being happy to hear an interesting thing, was more apt to throw it back at you. He was a very ugly man and he knew a lot of ugly words.

When the time had arrived for penitents to step forward and confess, Mr. Shostakovich, who had come to vespers with his wife, appeared anxious to get away. The town could only guess whether he had a premonition. Outside the sky was black. The saints were dancing on the windowpanes. Mrs. Shostakovich was heard to say to her husband, "It wouldn't do any harm for you to confess once in a while, Victor. You've got plenty to atone for, don't think you haven't."

Mr. Shostakovich had been holding onto his wife's arm. She gave him a poke in the ribs. He said that he believed he was coming down with a chill. All during vespers he had felt a draft blowing on his neck and he was afraid that if he didn't get home soon he was going to get sick. Besides that, he could not think of anything he had done wrong.

"Saint Victor—the perfect person," Mrs. Shostakovich said sarcastically. "Maybe someday they'll make a shrine in your honor and all the people can come."

Mr. Shostakovich was eighty-two years old. The dapper little mustache that had made him handsome when he was young looked now like a few snipped white threads under his nose, as if a seam had been pulled loose. In his Army days Mr. Shostakovich had been dashing and brave and very afraid to die. Countless nights he had stayed up until dawn drinking French wine with his comrades and losing countless rubles at cards and going to bed with prostitutes and once with a gypsy girl who turned out to be a boy. To all of these things he had confessed long ago, except for the sin with the boy, which he did not think should count since he had been deceived. There was also his sin with his wife Sofie, for whom he had deserted the Army and his country, but he felt he had more than made up for this by living with her these fifty-seven years.

Mrs. Shostakovich took her place where Father Alexey waited to hear the sins. Eight or nine other ladies stood in line. They all were of an age at which a person does not want to run the risk of carrying a major sin around on his soul for another week.

When Mrs. Shostakovich glanced over her shoulder to make sure Victor was there, he wasn't.

Mr. Shostakovich was headed home, down the snowy street. You could see him passing under the streetlamps, his shoulders pinched up against the wind. When he came out to the main street he stopped, looked up, and sniffed the air. In all the vast sky there was not a single star. A storm was coming. Mr. Shostakovich could smell it. He could feel it in his bones. He looked up the street toward his house. The porch light was on. He gave a shiver. "I'd better not go home without something to warm me up," he said. Crossing the street, he went down the alley to the kitchen door of the Hotel Nicholas the Second where his friend Smolnov worked.

Smolnov was a Cossack. Once a week he shaved his head, although hardly any hair grew on it anymore. He was bending over the sink, both arms deep in soapsuds, when Mr. Shostakovich peeked in the door. The cook was up front smoking a cigarette and talking to Lisaveta Stepanova, Smolnov's wife. She was a sad thin woman with pockets of blue under her eyes. She helped the cook and waited on tables and in between meals she cleaned rooms and the toilet upstairs and the one in the lobby and also was the maid for the owners, who lived on the top floor. The cook was stirring something in a pot. The dining room was quiet; with the weather turning bad, townspeople weren't going out.

When Smolnov saw Mr. Shostakovich, he gave a nod and Mr. Shostakovich went quietly into the storage room. In a little while Smolnov came back with their cups. From under a bag of soup bones in the freezer chest he dug out their bottle.

The vodka was as thick and smooth as syrup. It slid without a scratch down Mr. Shostakovich's throat and into his stomach. Then the warmth of it began to go out through his veins to every place his blood went and it made him feel warm and good.

Smolnov poured another two fingers into each of their cups. He put the bottle under the soup bones again in case the cook came in.

They leaned back in their chairs which they kept back there and took more time with the second one.

"Good health," said Smolnov, giving a salute with his cup.

He was a small, compact man with long lobey ears and teeth that clicked when he talked. It was easy to imagine him on a horse, fierce with his shaven head and a lance.

"Thank you, Gregor Mironovich. Long life to you."

"If you want more, just tell me," Smolnov said hospitably. The room smelled of flour and old wood. A little yellow bulb gave it mellow light and shadow. The heat from the kitchen helped to keep it cozy in winter. In the summer there was a window they could open and the breeze would bring them the smell of the pine forest from across the river.

Mr. Shostakovich sipped the vodka, trying to make it last. "I can't stay long," he said regretfully. "Sofie's confessing."

Smolnov said, "She's done something wrong, then."

Mr. Shostakovich shrugged. "I think she just likes to confess."

"She must have done something wrong," Smolnov said. "You can't tell the priest nothing. You've got to have a sin."

Mr. Shostakovich tried to think. "Sometimes she gets very impatient with me. I'm not sure if that counts or not."

"In *my* house I get respect," Smolnov said, although he did not have a house, he lived in a room upstairs with his wife.

"You should try to be nice to your husband if you're a woman, I think," Mr. Shostakovich said.

"Right in the beginning, they made a big mistake not putting it in the Ten Commandments," Smolnov said. "You've got to love your neighbor; you've got to honor your mother and father. But when it comes to husbands—nothing. I don't think it's right."

Mr. Shostakovich tried to remember the Commandments. It was a long time since he had had to recite them. He counted them on his fingers. Smolnov was right: There wasn't one about husbands. He said, "It's strange they left it out, isn't it?"

"If my wife makes trouble for me, she gets it right back," Smolnov said truculently.

"Mine, too," said Mr. Shostakovich.

"Women shouldn't try to boss people around," Smolnov said. "For one thing, their voices are too high."

"I'm sure Sofie isn't the only one who does it," Mr. Shostakovich said. "When I left there was a whole line of them waiting to confess."

Smolnov spat in a wastebasket. "If I were your wife I'd be careful where I told my sins. Those people don't go to confess, they go to listen. I wouldn't trust the priest, either."

"He seems very nice," Mr. Shostakovich said. "When Sofie had her gallstones out, he came to the hospital and sat for quite a long time by her bed. Maybe I'll have just one more cup. . . ."

"A Catholic!" Smolnov said with contempt.

Mr. Shostakovich did not like to disagree with his friend, especially when he seemed so sure of things. Mr. Shostakovich was rarely sure of anything, life was too confusing. He said, "I don't want to contradict you, Gregor Mironovich, but I've heard him say so himself: He used to be a Catholic but he converted. He thinks the Russian church adheres to the old values; that with the Catholics you don't know anymore what is a sin. That's what he said. Besides, if he didn't change, how could he be our priest?"

"Don't be naïve. How else can the Catholics infiltrate? Do you think the Pope is stupid? He's out to take over the whole thing."

Mr. Shostakovich did not think the Pope was stupid. But why should he be interested in the parish of Vasily the Blessed, which, at last count, was down to thirty-seven members? On the other hand, Smolnov had been in the Lubyanka prison and in one of Stalin's camps and he seemed to know a lot about plots.

Mr. Shostakovich looked out the window. The back porch light reached into the darkness, a small circle of light in the dark and cold night. He lifted his unfilled cup and let the single drop left in the bottom fall onto his tongue. Smolnov made no move to pour him another.

"Well, I'll just say good night, then," he said sadly. Pulling up his collar, he went out the door.

Sofie was waiting when he got home. He could tell from the way she stood with her hands on her hips that she was getting ready not to speak to him at some future point. He remembered, rather too late, to remove his rubbers so as not to leave puddles on the kitchen floor.

"So this is how you treat a chill," she said. She was standing in front of the cookstove, having already stoked it up and piled on new wood so that it was nice and warm.

"I'm glad you're home," Mr. Shostakovich said. "I was worried about you, Sofie. Out in this awful weather."

"Now I have to listen to lies as well!" There was a terribly angry look on her face. "Something I will never understand is how some people can let other people walk home alone in the dark in the middle of winter and maybe slip on the ice and break a hip and wind up in a nursing home. And then say they're worried!"

She went on to say other things. Mr. Shostakovich's thoughts began to drift. He heard her say something about "suffer the consequences" and "innocent people," and then it was not Sofie he was hearing but the mournful call to prayer from the minaret near the house in Sarajevo where they had lived after the war. He was seeing the mist on the river in the morning and smelling the fruit in the stalls. He could hear the joyful banter of the market women and the bells on the necks of the sheep.

"That's wonderful," Mrs. Shostakovich said. "I could be lying in a hospital somewhere and here he stands with a big smile on his face. It's very funny, isn't it?"

She marched into the bathroom and slammed the door. Almost immediately she opened it and said loudly, "All I know is that every day of my life I have to do things I don't feel like doing. But does anyone hear me complain?"

Mr. Shostakovich kept still. For many years he had conceded to his wife a kind of proprietary right over the last word and he had learned it was best not to do anything to delay its coming.

He put the kettle on for tea. Sofie was going on about the cross she had to bear. The kettle began to whistle, drowning her out. When Mr. Shostakovich removed it from the stove, Sofie's voice came through again so he put it back on for a while. Then he had the idea that a person might play a song that way, lifting a kettle on and off a fire, making it whistle a tune. For some moments he was absorbed in trying to do this—he was attempting "Hills of Manchuria Waltz," one of his favorites. When he looked around, Sofie was glaring at him.

"All right, Victor," she said in an injured way.

After she had gone to bed without saying good night, Mr. Shostakovich began to worry. Sometimes when Sofie stopped talking to him, she also stopped serving him meals, making him get up and get them himself from the stove.

"Tomorrow is church," he thought. "Maybe she just wants to get up early."

He lifted the top plate from the stove and stirred the coals. He remembered how in Sarajevo Sofie liked to rise early in the morning. They were married then, although they could not be sure whether her husband was alive or dead, but they presumed him to be the latter, for the killing in Russia at that time had been enormous.

He would watch her quietly dress and slip out the door. Soon she would return with fresh bread and fruit from the market and sometimes a pastry. He would smell the coffee cooking then, and she would sweeten it with honey and bring it to him with his breakfast on a tray and she would tell him about the snow on the tops of the mountains and the feel of the spring air with the sun slowly warming it. And he would lie contentedly in bed watching the mist rising from the river where he could see it from their window and he would be feeling very much for her, and for his life.

What had happened? He could not understand how everything had so completely changed. Sofie became round and lumpy. At some point her hands became strong and hard, like a stone mason's, and somehow the same thing, the hardness, had happened to her heart. Her veins made blue bumps on her legs. She liked to torment him.

"The cat's on the chair."

She might come in from the front room and say that.

But when he would ask on which chair the cat was, she would become annoyed and act as if he should know without her telling him or as if he had no right to know. In either case, she would not tell him.

"The only one he's on," she would say.

"Why can't you just tell me?"

"I don't like being interrogated."

Mr. Shostakovich liked to remember the way she had been

the night they met—beautiful and sad and waiting, he liked to think, for him, handsome and brave. It was in a provincial town where his regiment was garrisoned. The war had begun but the gentry still were having parties at their country estates. Sofie wore a black gown shining with a light that was either blue or green. It made him think of water in a well. She had come to the party with her husband, the commander of their regiment. He was an older man with sunken eyes and a bad stomach. On this night he was having some discomfort and left the party early. Sofie stayed. A lieutenant, an aide, was assigned to escort her home. The old man left upon his wife's cheek the kind of a kiss you might leave on the head of a child at bedtime.

It was summer. Sofie wandered onto the terrace. Without looking behind, somehow knowing he was there, she gazed up at the sky and as if speaking to the stars began to tell of a wood she knew where there was a hillside of wild berries and a path through tall ferns that brushed your arms as softly as feathers. The lieutenant stood near and smelled her perfume.

"Is it far away, this wood?"

She did not seem surprised to hear his voice so near.

"Yes," she said. "Far away, where I was young."

"You're young now," he said, laughing. He was young, too.

"No," she said. "I'm not young."

He watched her, the moonlight shining on her. He said, "Why don't you go back there, to this place?"

"It's gone." She looked at him then and tried to smile a little.

"A place? How can a place be gone?"

"I don't know. Like a person, maybe. One becomes lost."

"Maybe you'll see it again."

She shook her head. "I know I make it out to be more than it was," she said after a while. "But sometimes I dream of the path and the berries and then I am so happy that I wake up and then I begin to cry."

It was not possible for him not to love her.

What would his life have been, he often reflected, if Sofie's husband had not felt ill on that particular night? Or if in glancing around the room for an escort, the husband's eyes had fallen on another junior officer? Suppose Sofie had not stood under the stars? If he had not moved close enough to smell her perfume? If the ferns in her forest had not grown so tall as to brush against her slender white arms?

One thing Mr. Shostakovich knew, fate was determined not so much by God—frankly, people gave Him too much credit for things—as by dressmakers who sewed blue or green light into black cloth, by workmen who built terraces on which to stand on summer nights.

It was one reason why the world was so confusing, there being so many people doing so many arbitrary things without the slightest regard for their effect on people they didn't know, people maybe not even born yet, weaving countless fates into their random acts of obstinance and caprice and passion and maybe once in a while, logic. Destiny was left all a tangle, like a ball of string the cat had got at, so that you couldn't tell where the thread began or where it left off but one thing was certain—it was all connected.

And what of Russia? He did not mean to be immodest, but weren't they weavers in their own right? Their running away together must have aggravated the ulcer of Sofie's husband terrifically. Later, when the Russians had turned from fighting the Germans and Austrians to fighting themselves, Sofie's husband held an important position on General Kornilov's staff. With a more tranquil stomach, would he have thought up a plan for reconnoitering the Bolshevik lines? Proposed a better way of bringing up supplies from the rear? Mr. Shostakovich could imagine from his own occasional bowel discomfort that how you feel in your stomach can make a world of difference in how well you draw up strategies.

On the other hand, if they hadn't run away he might have been killed—and what was the good in that? If not on the field of battle, then against some bloody wall or, worse, in one of the forced-labor camps. Then where would Sofie be? It wasn't that she wouldn't be able to get by without him: Lately she amazed him with her ability to open jars whose lids had frozen shut, to carry in firewood without straining her back. He doubted, however, that on her own she would have dinner ready at a regular hour or that she would remember to put tools back in the shed where a person could find them. Also she did not like to empty the cat litter even though she had promised she would do that when they got the cat. She probably would buy a lot of worthless things at lawn sales.

Mr. Shostakovich awoke from his thoughts to find himself staring into ashes as insubstantial as air. His stirring had brought up the fire, but now it was gone. He probed around with the poker, looking for a coal. He tried blowing but the ashes flew up in his eyes and he couldn't see. He put the plate back on the stove and went upstairs to bed.

In the morning when he awoke, Sofie was not in bed. A meager light at the window suggested daylight. Mr. Shostakovich put on his robe and opened the shade. It was snowing. A limb that had broken from the locust tree in the front yard was turned by the snow into a creature with monstrous arms and claws. The fire hydrant on the corner had sprouted a bulbous nose and comical ears. The garbage can was a tower, the woodpile a mountain.

Looking out, Mr. Shostakovich saw Sofie going down the front steps. It seemed early for her to be going to church. The snow was up to her knees and when she reached the gate she stopped and for a long while stood holding onto the post as if to catch her breath. As he watched, Mr. Shostakovich started to feel badly. It was not nice, what he had done with the kettle. Suddenly he had a dreadful thought: What if Sofie were to die before she got back? He visualized her in church lighting a candle before the ikon of St. Vasily, then having a seizure of some kind and falling over dead.

What a fuss there would be!—people running around, not knowing what to do, the service being interrupted while some of the men carried Sofie's body across the street to Payson's Funeral Home. Mr. Shostakovich saw himself at the graveside, throwing in his shovel of dirt. People always came to funerals with big appetites. They would want a meal afterwards. How could he be expected to cook for so many people?

Suddenly Mr. Shostakovich realized that not only did he not know how to cook, he didn't know how to work the washing machine. Sofie did something with the dials on top but just what, he was uncertain. And what was the telephone number of the man who brought their firewood? Sofie always called him about now, before the ground in the forest thawed and became mud.

He decided he had better get dressed and go see if she was all right.

Mr. Shostakovich hurriedly pulled on his trousers and

went downstairs and got into his galoshes and coat and winter hat. He was at the front door when he remembered his scarf: Sofie would scold if he went out without it. Returning to the hall closet, Mr. Shostakovich smelled coffee cooking. He looked into the kitchen. On the counter by the sink the electric coffee pot was perking. On the table his place was set with his cup and dish and spoon.

"She isn't angry!" Mr. Shostakovich cried joyfully. With a feeling of great relief, he took off his coat and hat and galoshes. He looked at the clock on the wall. Probably, he thought, she had gone out to buy some buns at the store. He set out a place for her, and also butter and jam for the buns. As he waited for Sofie to return, he drank two cups of coffee and ate two pieces of toast because he was getting hungry.

Then he had an odd sense of fear. He looked at his hands. They were shaking. He felt his heart. It seemed to be beating faster than it should. Something, he was sure, had happened to Sofie. On rubbery legs he reached the hall closet and again got into his hat and coat and galoshes and again forgot his scarf. Opening the front door, he squinted into the snow and called Sofie's name.

Then he went into the storm, scuffing forward to the gate, following Sofie's tracks which now were only shallow indentations in the snow.

Just outside, on the sidewalk, he came upon a mound of snow that somehow made him think of the Caucasus. With his mittened hand, Mr. Shostakovich cleared the snow off the highest hill. It was Sofie's hip.

"You shouldn't be lying here like this, Sofie," he said, brushing downwards until he saw her eyes blinking up at him. "You're going to get sick."

He made her sit by the stove and put her feet in a basin with Epsom salts.

"You gave me a fright," he said. "You know what the doctor said about my heart."

"I'm sorry, Victor." Sorry was not a word he was used to hearing from her.

"*Now* you're sorry," he said, surprised at his own reproachful tone. "You should think about these things beforehand."

Her silence made him uneasy.

Later, when he had her feet in his lap and was drying them with a towel, she said, "Victor, why do you live in dreams?"

"I don't live in dreams."

"Don't say that, Victor. I've seen you. You drift away. I look at you and I think, 'Where is he now?' "

"Would you like me to do your toenails for you, Sofie? They've softened up nicely."

"Do you hear what I say, Victor?"

"Of course I hear what you say."

"You think there's happiness in the world. You think it's somewhere like a country on a map, that all you have to do is cross the border and you'll be there, and you'll be happy. That's one dream. You think that General Kornilov might still be alive, that all this while he has been hiding out in the Caucasus, waiting for the right moment to march on Moscow and throw out the Communists. Don't deny it— I've heard you say it."

"I never said it. Only that it's possible."

"And what you think of me. That's another dream."

She waited for him to say something.

"You think I'm a good person," she said.

"You are a good person, Sofie."

"I'm not. You only think it."

Mr. Shostakovich looked down at his wife's feet in his lap. Her toenails were round and yellow like kernels of corn. "Sofie—"

"Not again, Victor." She knew the tone—that infuriatingly fond and tender tone—knew at once that he now would start on the fond old things.

"I was just thinking," he said. She could have mouthed it: "I was just thinking of the gown you wore . . . the terrace . . . how I followed . . . "

"Victor," she said. "I didn't fall."

". . . how you never looked around and just started to speak up at the sky. Suppose it had been another man behind you? I wonder, Sofie—would you have loved him, too?"

"I didn't fall," she repeated.

He looked at her for a moment—as if to look longer would be like looking directly at the sun. It could burn you, the sun. But he did not immediately retreat, either, as was his custom, retreating before potential trouble into his redoubt of old age and bafflement where nothing would harm or disturb him, where nothing could be expected of him—not action, not answers.

Sofie saw this. She said, "The gown is gone, Victor."

"It was a beautiful gown," he said. To her surprise, he bent suddenly and kissed one of the bumpy blue veins in her bare leg.

"So is that night and the terrace and all of it, including Russia, including Kornilov," she said unmercifully. "They are all gone. You know that, don't you?"

He was not looking, not saying anything.

"You can't think, Victor, that anything will ever remain

what it was. Only death does that, and death isn't something, it's nothing. You can't think that people won't do awful things and knowing they're awful do them just the same. We can't help it, we don't know enough to know what else to do. Do you understand what I'm saying? It's hard for me to explain, Victor. You've got to help me now."

But it was too late. He had been brave for as long as he could. Sofie closed her eyes so that she would not see it.

Rising, he set her feet carefully on the seat of his chair.

"Now you just stay here where it's nice and warm," he said. "And I'll find the scissors and do those nails."

In the doorway he stopped.

"You *are* a good person, Sofie," he said.

And then he tottered out.

Mrs. Shostakovich missed church that day. "Victor," she kept saying. "Come here and sit down."

He tried to avoid her as best he could. When she walked into a room, he walked out. He traveled from window to window, upstairs and down, to look out at the storm. He searched for something in the attic. At lunchtime he said he wasn't hungry and went to putter in the shed. At dinner time he took his plate into the living room and turned on the television.

He knew it was going to be something bad. She didn't fall—what could that mean? She had told him not to think of the terrace, the gown, the moonlight. They were gone, she said. He tried to think of Sarajevo. She had not said not to think of that. But it was hard to do it and to keep an eye out for Sofie, who might enter a room at any time.

When it was time for bed, Mr. Shostakovich stayed downstairs checking the back and front doors several times to make sure they were locked. He unplugged the television so that lightning, if it struck the antenna on the roof, would not come in through the plug and burn the house down. He made sure the cellar door was left ajar for the cat to get to her litter box. He pushed with all his strength on the cold water tap in the bathroom, but it still dripped. He made sure the rope was securely in place around the refrigerator door in case it decided to pop open during the night and ruin their food.

Finally, he came up. Sofie was in bed. She watched as he methodically tucked his socks into his shoes, draped his trousers over the back of the chair, and laid out his underwear for the next day. When he at last had on his pajamas, she said, "Victor, I have to tell you something."

"I thought I might read a little."

"You don't have to read tonight."

Mr. Shostakovich looked at the clock. "My God, it's already ten-thirty!" he said. "We'd better get to sleep or we'll never get up in the morning!"

"Victor, I'm asking you."

Mr. Shostakovich got into bed and turned out the light. Right away, he made believe he was asleep. He faked a snore.

"Victor!"

"What is it, Sofie?" He tried to sound angry. "I was sound asleep."

"Victor, I . . ." But now she could not tell him. Every time she tried to speak, a sigh came out instead. Outside, the snow had ended. The wind had blown the sky clear. The moonlight was on the windowshade. A faint glow crept into the room. Sofie could see Victor's face quite clearly. He looked as if he were about to be given a needle at the doctor's. She closed her eyes.

And then she told him of her second sin.

For a long time Mr. Shostakovich did not make a sound or say a word or even move a little. When Sofie looked, she thought that maybe he had died, as she had feared he might, of a heart attack. His eyes were open and fixed, his body rigid under the quilt, his face blue in the bluish light.

"Victor, I didn't intend for it to happen." She saw his chest rise.

"Didn't . . . ," he said.

"I only went out to do some shopping. It was a long time ago, Victor. We were still living in New York. And I went out shopping one day. Afterward, I stopped for a cup of tea. . . ."

"Tea . . . "

"And he came in. How could I have known? We thought he was dead. And I was just having a cup of tea because it was a cold day and I think I had a slice of some kind of a torte, I can't remember exactly, and then I heard him say my name and when I looked up I almost died. I thought he was a ghost. I couldn't believe what I was seeing."

She felt his sigh in the moon-lightened dark. It was like a last breath.

"And what did you say?" The words were almost without wanting to know, flat and dead.

"I told you, it was a long time ago."

"You must have said something."

"Of course I said something."

"Well, when did you do it?" he said nastily. "You couldn't have done it there in the restaurant."

"Don't be like that, Victor."

"Me?" he said. "*Me?*"

"All right, Victor. What do you want me to do?"

"You want to tell me. I want to know. Tell me, then. I want to hear it."

Mrs. Shostakovich closed her eyes. She said, "He had a room. It wasn't far away."

"And how was it?"

She did not answer.

"All of a sudden, you don't want to talk about it?"

"Victor," she said. She felt very tired. "Believe me, it has been like a stone on my heart."

"And now you've given it to me."

"I know. I didn't want to."

For a long time they lay side by side, far from each other, and did not say anything. There was only the room, the faint light from the moon, the sound of their breathing. When he climbed from the bed, Sofie thought that perhaps it was only to go to the bathroom. Instead he sat and began to lace on his shoes.

"Where are you going?"

He did not answer.

Finally, she said, "Victor, he was my husband. And I had never said good-bye."

His shoe struck the wall above the bed. Mrs. Shostakovich pulled the quilt over her head in case he threw the other one. Then she heard him on the stairs, going down as fast as he could, the one foot with the shoe clumping on every other step. The front door slammed.

Sofie rose and put on her housecoat. Downstairs, the door of the hall closet was open. His coat was gone.

"Now," she thought, "it's his turn to kill himself."

She looked in the closet to see if he had remembered to take his scarf.

Mr. Shostakovich also had forgotten his galoshes and his hat. Pretty soon his ears started to get cold and so did his foot without the shoe. He crossed the street to the hotel. It was late. The dining room was closed. A few old people who lived in the rooms upstairs were snoring in front of the television in the lobby. The late night news was on. Mr. Shostakovich rang the bell at the desk. This caused one old man who was sleeping to wake up. He nudged awake his neighbors.

Mr. Shostakovich rang the bell again. From the kitchen he heard a curse word. A shaven head appeared at the window of the kitchen door.

Not having on a shoe made Mr. Shostakovich stand a little lop-sided. Right away Smolnov noticed this.

"Good evening, Gregor Mironovich," said Mr. Shostakovich. "I'd like a room, please."

"What happened to your shoe?"

"What shoe are you talking about?"

"What shoe do you think? The one that's not on your foot."

Mr. Shostakovich looked down. The snow between his toes was starting to melt. "I must have forgotten it," he said, drying his foot against the leg of his pajamas.

"It must have been some fight!" Smolnov said with relish. By now the news of the confession had reached him. "If you ask me, she's the one who should have been thrown out."

"Sofie didn't throw me out," Mr. Shostakovich said. "I decided to leave, that's all. We're probably going to get a divorce."

Leaning over the desk, Smolnov lowered his voice. "Do you know yet who it was? I heard she did it twice."

The old man in the chair who had been the first to wake up said, "I saw her talking with Ivan Melnik in the store the other day."

"Ivan Melnik used to be very popular with the ladies," said the old woman in the chair next to him.

"Sofie gave him a big smile," the man said. "I was right there."

"Do you know who is looking for a woman?" said a second old man. "Father Vladimir. They say that since his wife died he's been as lonely as a finger."

"I don't think Sofie would have an adultery with him," the first old man said as if he knew. "For one thing, they're in opposite churches."

"That doesn't mean a thing nowadays," the old woman said.

"Well, there's a second one somewhere," said the man who had thought of Father Vladimir.

"Gregor Mironovich," Mr. Shostakovich said. "Please give me a room."

"I don't check people in." Smolnov lifted his chin to indicate the upstairs where lived the owners. "The big shots do that."

"Please, Gregor Mironovich. I can't go home now."

"Do you want me to get in trouble?"

"Life is trouble. I've heard you say so many times. You're a Cossack. What's trouble to a Cossack?"

Smolnov considered this for a moment, then pulled the registration book from under the counter. "Ten dollars," he said.

"For just one night?"

"It's cheaper by the week. You want to stay a week?"

"I'm not sure yet. Maybe I will, maybe I won't."

"They don't have a rate for longer than a week," said Smolnov. "They can't be sure anyone around here will last that long." The two old men and the old woman in the chairs looked away guiltily.

"I'll just take the one night," Mr. Shostakovich said. "But I think it's very expensive."

"Tell their majesties. Any luggage?"

Mr. Shostakovich shook his head. "I'm having it forwarded," he said.

He unbuttoned his overcoat and searched his pajamas.

"I seem to have misplaced my billfold."

"Your billfold?" said Smolnov. "You don't even have a pocket."

"I can pay you tomorrow."

"Victor Konstantinovich, you ought to be better prepared," Smolnov said disapprovingly. "How are you going to get a divorce if you can't even remember to wear your trousers when you go out at night?" He threw the room key on the counter, as if disgusted with his friend.

Mr. Shostakovich looked at the key for a while, as if it were an item he was considering buying.

"Maybe I'll just stay down here a bit," he said.

"Suit yourself, but in ten minutes I'm going to put out the lights. You people are going to have to go up, too," Smolnov said to the ones in the chairs.

"I'll just have a cup of tea, perhaps," Mr. Shostakovich said.

"There's no tea," Smolnov said. "The kitchen's closed." In a softened tone, he added, "You can have your tea in the morning."

Mr. Shostakovich looked at Smolnov with woeful eyes.

"Are you sure you'd rather not just go home?" Smolnov asked.

Mr. Shostakovich slowly shook his head. "I don't think I can, Gregor Mironovich. I'm afraid I've left."

It was a long climb up the stairs. Mr. Shostakovich listened for a voice that would call him back. None came. All he heard was one of the old men in the chairs ask, "Where did he say he left his shoe?"

The hallway at the top was lit by a dim light outside the toilet door. As he passed under it, Mr. Shostakovich saw the shells of hundreds of bugs entombed inside its globe. From the toilet came a stale, airless smell. Then the floor seemed to move and he had the sense that by some device time and the world had rotated under his feet and he was being led to a place where he had been before and the smell was a part of it.

In this place was no summer night, no terrace on which to stand with Sofie, no river with its feathered mist. Yet he went along into it. He was quite alert. He knew it was not a dream because it was not sleep or longing that had brought him here but his own willful act of climbing step by step up a steep stair and venturing down a dark hall, into the darkening, into the smell of death. Once he had been a soldier who had run away. If he had been Sofie's lover, he had also been her coward. How could you expect a woman to be faithful to a coward? Now he was back to where he had started. He could hear the gunfire now. He had not expected to find this chance again.

His outstretched hand touched a wall. Was that the indent of a bullet? Was that the smell of blood? A door opened. The light blinked on in a room. Mr. Shostakovich stepped in bravely, expecting here to find the ghosts before which he would not tremble, before which he would declare he had not deserted because he was afraid. But there was only an empty room, a narrow bed, a pasteboard dresser, a sink on which lay a thin piece of pink soap.

The room was ice cold. Mr. Shostakovich sat on the bed

with his coat on and began to cry. With every little movement, the springs creaked. "This is your fault, Sofie," he said. He wiped his tears on his sleeve. He felt that his nose was very cold. He bent over and felt the toes of his shoeless foot.

I'd better get in bed, he thought, before I catch pneumonia. He turned down the covers, then went to the window to close the shade. Up the street he could see his house. The light was on in the bedroom. As he watched, he thought he saw Sofie looking out.

Mr. Shostakovich waved wildly.

"Sofie!" he cried. "It's me!"

He was waving both arms. He was certain he saw the figure at the window wave back.

"It's Sofie, all right," he said.

Pretty soon his arms got tired waving. He felt sleepy. He gave one more wave and went back to the bed, spreading his coat out over the top of it. When he got under the covers, the sheet was damp. His toes started to ache. From the pockets of his overcoat he took his mittens and pulled them over his feet. After a while, they felt better. He began to feel warm all over. He closed his eyes. The branch of a tree scratched at the windowpane. He imagined it was Sofie trying to comfort him, scratching on his window the way she scratched their cat on the neck.

Tomorrow, he thought, she would bring him his shoe or he would borrow one from Smolnov and then he could go home. Sofie would have been greatly worried, and so she would be happy to have him back. She would make him get straight into bed. And then she would fix his breakfast and bring it up to him and he would ask her to sweeten his coffee with honey, the way she used to do it in Sarajevo.

Mr. Shostakovich turned on his side. He was smiling. Almost at once he began to sleep. Almost at once he began to dream.

heir
to
the
realm

By the time the old woman made her entrance, the choir of
the Church of Vasily the Blessed was running out of songs.
   There were four ladies and two gentlemen left in the choir—
others in town who could carry a tune had, unfortunately,
died—and each Sunday before the service began they sang
some opening numbers. Their place was right up front, to
one side of the ikonostasis. Nothing was more embarrassing

on a Sunday morning than being out front where everyone could see you, and to be running out of songs.

And so they were nervous and making mistakes. The old woman was late, and the priest was not beginning without her. Mr. Leonov, the director, had started the choir on a song it had not practiced for a long time. He was getting irritated, probably because he was nervous, too. Twice he stopped directing, put his hands on his hips, and acted fed up. The choir members were looking desperately toward the door to see if the old woman had arrived yet. Mr. Leonov, who was proud, would not look around for anything.

But the old woman did not hurry. She did not seem to notice the song any more than she seemed to know or care about the hour or notice the skirts of Father Alexey behind the ikonostasis where he stood waiting to come out.

She came through the door like a shadow making room for the sun, drifting the way shadows do, displacing in her black dress the bit of light in the vestibule where she stopped to buy her candles. The people looked around and saw her there carefully counting out her coins from a knotted hand-kerchief. Automatically they turned to see the face of Maxim Maximovich's wife. She also would have been watching so that she would know when not to look.

Maxim Maximovich's wife was a woman who had every-thing—new clothes, a nice place to live, money enough not to worry about paying the oil bill, real hairdos from the hairdresser's. Also, she was still young, only in her fifties. So the people when they looked did not mind at all seeing her with her eyes shut harder than in actual prayer, the strain of composure showing on her face, her grip tightening on the thin arm of her daughter, Sonya, who once had mortified her by curtsying to the old woman.

They saw her giving the arm a jerk to keep the girl looking straight ahead.

The people could not say why they assumed the old woman to be something more than Maxim Maximovich's wife, who had always been pre-eminent in the town. Certainly, no one had ever heard the old woman speak of being high-born or even speaking in a high-born manner, had hardly ever heard her speak at all. To church she always wore a hat with a veil, so there were plenty of people who did not even know what she looked like, other than like a kind of darkness, a shadow. She lived alone in an old farmhouse on the Annabessacook Road, the house and the barn both sagging where the sills were rotted. The name on the mailbox was written in wavery letters, the way an old woman's hand might be expected to write, and it said *Anna Rus*. People believed there was more to the name than that, and they figured she had just run out of room, or paint, or maybe the strength to write the rest of it in, being very old. Anyhow, the name, even that fragment, did not seem to be anything more than common, so it must have been something else.

The farmer who had the place next door brought her to town in his old red truck when she needed to come. She paid him each time. People said she looked as if she were riding in a royal carriage, sitting up so erect and grand, passing by without so much as a glance in anyone's direction. So maybe it was that. Or maybe it was her unhurried step across any sort of threshold, as if she were not answerable to any time or schedule other than her own. Or maybe it had to do with the time in the grocery store when Krenko, the dissident, who had very little respect for older people, came along the aisle and called her Your Highness, his kind of a joke. Instead of giving him the dirty look he deserved, the old woman abandoned her shopping basket and hurried out of the store, and the people who were there told about the look on her face.

Those were the only times she came to town, to go to church or to the market or once in a while to the post office, speaking no more than the few words necessary to find an item on the store shelf or buy a stamp and then on Sunday arriving at church at her own time, lighting her sixty cents' worth of candles before the ikon of St. Vasily and then leaving early—the farmer blowing his horn when he had finished his various errands (which usually included having a drink with the boys at the gas station)—and not having to speak at all.

There were any number of places to go in town—the laundromat, the bank, the variety store; or you could sit on a bench by the river. Old people seemed to like to do that—watch the river go by. There also was the Hotel Nicholas the Second, which Maxim Maximovich's wife owned. It was more of a boarding house than a hotel, but they had a public dining room and on nice afternoons ladies liked to have a cup of tea and a pastry out on the veranda. If you knew one of the residents, you could visit and watch a show on the color television in the lobby. So there were plenty of places where a person could go, different things to do, but the old woman didn't do any of them, just lived out there alone on that country lane.

Except for funerals. Funerals she almost never missed. Not only did she go to the ones at Vasily the Blessed, but to those at the Holy Virgin of Kazan, the rival church, and even to the ones at the Ukrainian Autocephalic Orthodox Holy Cross Elevation Church, where they didn't like Russians very much, particularly those who thought Russians and Ukrainians were the same thing.

And this was another thing the town could not figure: why an old woman choosing to live the life of a recluse should decide it was necessary to come into town to kiss in their coffins people she had never bothered to glance at when they were alive. Most of their names she could not even have known, having lived only a couple of years in the house on the Annabessacook Road. Where she had lived before, no one knew. That also was hard to figure because people had moved into town from all over the world—from South River, New Jersey; Brooklyn, New York; from more than one country in South America—and no one had ever run into her in any of those places, either.

When it was time to close the lid on the casket, the old woman would step forward through the cloud of incense and raise her veil. It was then that people could see her face, see that the grief on it was not just something worn for the occasion. She would bend and kiss the hands and the head, as is the custom. But near the head she would linger, and she would be seen to whisper into the dead person's ear. It was something more than a prayer—something that took some time to tell.

At Mr. Kaputin's funeral, Mrs. Florenskaya, approaching the coffin, found the old woman's tears still wet on the corpse's face.

"Praise God, it's a miracle!" she screamed, scaring everyone half to death. "Poor Yakov! Just look, he's crying! I think it's because he hates to leave us!"

At the cemetery the old woman would stand off a little way, waiting for them to begin shoveling in the dirt. Then she would climb back into the red truck—sometimes the farmer's wife or their boy would be driving—and they would take her home and she would be sitting up erect and dignified and not looking at anyone again.

It must have been hard on Maxim Maximovich's wife, being only a baroness, thinking of all she had done for the town in terms of providing its older citizens with a roof over their heads at the Nicholas the Second and looking after their Social Security checks and the estates of those who had passed on and then having maybe a countess, maybe something more, usurping her standing, knowing all along that it was her husband, Maxim Maximovich, who had sold her the house on the Annabessacook Road. It must have been harder still that in church, where one came to nourish the soul, that she should suffer the humiliation of having to wait like an ordinary person and then to feel the attention, the deference, which had always been hers in the town, being drawn away inexorably at the old woman's entrance.

Of course, it was not only the old woman—the people understood that. It was the two of them: the old woman and the child. And the baroness each Sunday having to stand between the two of them with the people watching to see how she would act.

Sonya was twelve years old. In some places in the world, a girl when she is twelve is ready to be a bride. Sonya was ready for almost nothing in life. She was the merest child. You could never say of her, ''One day she will be . . .'' because you had the sense that she would never be more than she was now. Her mother tried to make her pretty by dressing her in pink dresses and putting ribbons in her hair. She made her wear white gloves and carry a dainty purse. None of it helped. Sonya remained homely and thin with hair of no definite color and a face that looked as if her blood did not circulate there.

She had turned out funny in ways other than her looks. For one thing, she was jumpy, worse than ants in the pants.

For another, she had a habit of repeating words and whole sentences—not a stutter, but a repeat. She had an idea that when she grew up she would be a priest. She seemed to like it that on certain feast days, if you were a priest, you could wear a crown. She practiced looking like Father Alexey, going around the town and in the corridors at school holding her long colorless curls under her chin to make a beard. Her schoolmates called her Rasputin. "Watch out, here comes Crazy Rasputin!" they shrieked when they saw her.

In her room she held regular church services before the ikons, serving communion to her dolls. At intervals she would signal to the picture of the Tsar on her dresser, pretending that he was Mr. Palchinsky, the church warden, letting him know when it was time to collect the money. The Tsarina became Mrs. Golitsyn, who sold the candles. Photographs of the five children were tacked up on the wall. They were Sonya's choir.

"Are you ready, Marie?" she would say. "How about you, Olga? Alexey, be still! Look at me, everyone. All together now, sing!"

From the doctor the baroness got pills to try to cure Sonya's jumps. For her repeats and for her priestly ambitions he could prescribe nothing except for Sonya to spend more time with boys and girls her own age. But to play with American children, the baroness felt, would place her daughter in danger of adopting wild ways, such as yelling down the street, wearing blue jeans, saying swear words, and smoking cigarettes or—God forbid—marijuana.

The doctor's pills worked no better than his advice. At the slightest reprimand or reproving look, sometimes at a mere question, Sonya started. It was as if keeping on the move, keeping the words coming, would keep her out of danger.

One day into the face of Mrs. Bukharin, who was visiting, she blurted, "Pity poor Yakov," over and over. When her mother told her in very definite words to stop it, she repeated that, "Stop it Sonya, stop it stop it stop it." She got slapped good for it. Tears in her eyes, holding onto the sting in her arm, she ran off to her bedroom, sobbing, "Naughty girl, naughty girl who wants to shame her mother."

On Sundays, Maxim Maximovich went off to show the houses and farms he had for sale, so it was always her mother who took Sonya to church. They stood on the right side, under the stained glass window that the baroness had donated. On it was a picture of the warrior saint Alexander Nevsky sitting on a great white horse, his sword dripping with the blood of the Teutonic knight whose head he had just lopped off. Underneath was the family name and the legend DON'T TREAD ON MOTHER RUSSIA.

One Sunday during the service Sonya felt sleepy. She closed her eyes. Her head tilted, touching her mother's side. At once she awoke and—afraid she was going to get hit—began to jump. To her surprise, her mother put her arm around her. Maybe it was only because people were there to see, but anyhow she did not get hit. Her mother even held her quite close.

The next Sunday, as an experiment, Sonya tried it again, inclining her head to her mother's side. Again it happened: The arm went up, went around her, pulled her in close. It made Sonya grin.

The best part about being held like this, she discovered, was that her mother's bosom was a high one and it stuck way out, making a kind of ledge. Under it, unobserved from above, Sonya could gaze to her heart's content across the church at the old woman.

She soon made another discovery. If she looked without blinking while counting slowly to ten, all the while putting the wishing of her heart into it, she could reach out with her sight as with her hand, and the old woman would feel it.

The very first time she tried this, the face across the church began to turn in her direction. For maybe a minute or more they looked at each other in silence, the one hidden under her mother's bosom, the other behind the shadow of her veil. Sonya at first blinked and twitched, as if getting ready to do some serious jumping. Then, as though suddenly she saw in the unseen face something utterly reassuring, utterly unfearsome—as if she had been gazing into a shadowy place in the river at the moment the sun struck through, revealing a safe and sandy bottom—Sonya relaxed and began to smile. The face turned back. Sonya believed that beneath the veil it was smiling, too.

Then it was just a matter of learning to speak without words, of learning the secret of putting the words of your heart into the palm of your hand and, being careful not to let any spill, gently blowing, sending them off like seeds that sail on the wind.

It's Sunday, Grandmother, Sonya would remind her. She had taken to calling her that.

And the old woman would say, *It's your turn today, child. You choose. Where shall we go?*

And maybe if it were summer and hot in the little church, Sonya would say with delight: *The winter place!*

Outside the church the sleigh would be waiting. It was bright red, like the farmer's truck. They galloped down the hill, across the river, through the forest, the runners whistling over the snow. The driver had a jug beside him on the seat and when he drank from it he began to shout and sing. He cracked his whip over the heads of the horses—and they flew!

The children would be waiting. The three older girls looked sad, just as in the pictures on Sonya's wall. Sonya liked better the smallest girl, Anastasia, who wore a party dress and golden slippers, as if she were going to church with her mother. She also liked the boy, Alexey, who dressed in a sailor suit and had a pony.

The girls would show Sonya their rooms and their clothes and dolls. Then all of them, including their father, the Tsar, would take turns riding the pony round and round a room in the palace whose walls were hung with mirrors as high as the ceiling, so that as they rode, wherever they looked, they saw ecstatic faces. It was as if a crowd of people had turned out with great joy to see them at play. They waved and the people waved back, their faces filled with happiness.

But always then—always when they were having the most fun—always the horn had to blow. It was the driver in his sleigh. He would have been drinking all this time and he blew his horn rudely, as if he didn't care for a thing. Sonya shut her eyes and shut her ears to keep the noise away. But always when she opened them, the old woman would be gone. And so would be the dream.

At the church services she held in her room, Sonya said special prayers for Sunday to hurry. Each morning when she got out of bed, she looked at the calendar to see the day and count the number left until the day with the red number. But mostly Sunday seemed to come of its own accord, at its own time, moving the way shadows do.

This Sunday came that way, arriving at the end of a dreary night when the rain blew against the windowpane and Sonya lay awake in her bed, rising from time to time to look out and see if dawn had started yet. In the morning, dark clouds covered the sky. The clumps of snow remaining along the roadside looked like sheep standing in the rain—about that forlorn, about that dirty.

But it was spring. As her mother hurried with her down the rainy street, Sonya saw a mist of green floating over the branches of a tree. Close to the foundation of a house shoots as delicate and pale of life as anything just born broke through the crust of the earth. The raindrop that fell on Sonya's wrist as she held out her hand was a warm one.

In church the people prayed a little and gossiped a little, standing easy as they waited for the service to begin. The choir was struggling with an unfamiliar song but the people did not seem to notice so much. Milk and meat and butter had appeared on their tables again after the long Lenten fast and life was not such a hard thing now.

Sonya and her mother went to their place under their window. When Sonya saw the people glancing over, she knew that the old woman had arrived. Then she got her arm jerked. She moved in under the bosomy ledge and waited, looking out. She saw the old woman coming up through the congregation. The old woman went to the ikon and lighted her six candles. When she had gone to her spot across from where they stood, the priest came out and started the service—much to the relief of the choir and its director, Mr. Leonov.

They chose this day the summer place. It was a house built of gleaming white stone and it stood in a warm land high on a hill overlooking a warm sea. The driver took them up in his red wagon. Sonya found herself on a balcony surrounded by flowers and plants with leaves as big as sails. In the distance, by the sea, was a village whose houses were all the colors of the flowers of the garden. From the slant of their shadows, Sonya could see that the light that lit the town did not come directly from the sun but from where she stood, from the house on the hill. The sun lit the house, and the house lit up the world.

Look, Grandmother, she said. But when she turned, the old woman, as usual, was gone.

Standing in her place were the five children and their father and mother.

See, children, here's your Sonya, the mother said.

The smallest girl, Anastasia, said, *We've been waiting an awfully long time.*

The boy said, *Do you want to go sailing on the sea?*

But Olga, who was the oldest, said, *First, we're having our picnic.*

The father carried their lunch in a basket. Today he was wearing a sailor's suit, too. One of the girls brought a cooler with lemonade, the ice jiggling wonderfully inside. They spread a cloth on the green grass on the side of the hill. They could see the glittering sea and all around them the world with its flowers and sunshine. Sonya hoped the driver would not come soon and blow his awful horn.

Instead, she felt a sharp tug on her arm.

"Hey, wake up!" she heard her mother say. "Are you sleeping?"

Sonya opened her eyes. She was back in the church. The service was over. People were leaving. But when she looked over, the old woman was still there. The farmer had not come for her. This had never happened before.

The old woman was staring straight ahead, upright and rigid as a flagpole. But now in the stiff back, in the high head that not once in anyone's memory had nodded or inclined in any manner to suggest the merest acknowledgment of the presence of anyone—in this now was not pride or remoteness but something that had the appearance of fear. She looked as if suddenly she had been abandoned in a place she did not know, among people who might be unkind.

The congregation was moving slowly toward the door. The people kept glancing back, keeping an eye on the old woman and also on the baroness to see what she might do. The old woman took a step in toward the ikon where her candles burned, as if she would be one step safer there.

The baroness was not waiting to see anything; she had Sonya by the hand, pulling her along like a shopping cart.

Grandmother! Sonya cried in the way that was their secret, with words that no one else could hear.

"First I catch you sleeping," the baroness said angrily, giving Sonya a shake. "Now you don't know how to walk. Do you hear me? I said, come along!"

When they arrived at their apartment on the top floor of the Nicholas the Second, Sonya without pause went to her room where she was told she belonged for the remainder of the day for dragging on her mother's arm the whole way home from church and not listening when told to stop it.

The baroness, for her part, went to the kitchen and poured herself a glass of wine.

It went quickly to her head. She rather hoped it would. She carried the bottle into the living room. Sitting on the divan, she slipped off her shoes and put her toes into the deepness of the carpet. Around her were her candelabra, her mahogany table, her porcelain figurines, the wallpaper with the real velvet in it. Looking from one of these to another, she began to feel herself restored to her position in the world.

Ever since her pregnancy, the baroness had been trying

not to be fat. She wore a girdle and other undergarments to hold in her stomach and other parts. When she could get out of bed in time, she did the morning exercises along with the slender young ladies who showed you how to do them on the television. Now, catching sight of herself in the glass of the cabinet that held her silver and good dishes, she observed with satisfaction that she still had a figure with shape left in it. She guessed she could pass for someone in her forties, maybe even late thirties. And here she was, almost fifty-two! Even now, she did not have gray in her hair except for the few strands which she had been coloring because it hurt to keep pulling them out.

This might be the reason, the baroness thought, that the old woman did not look at her in church. It probably was more than she could stand—to see somebody who was young and with a good figure and advantaged in so many other ways. The old woman would be knowing, for instance, that if the baroness wanted to go somewhere she did not have to beg a ride in a farmer's old red truck. And if one ever wanted to compare houses, one had only to start by driving out the Annabessacook Road, as the baroness had done many times, and taking a look at the tin roof with the rust streaking down from the nail holes, the ridiculous tarpaper that was supposed to look like bricks, the grass growing down the middle of the driveway.

"There I go again," the baroness said, catching herself. "Now I'm starting to feel sorry for her."

It was a big weakness of hers, feeling sorry for people who didn't appreciate it. But she couldn't help it, having been born, apparently, with more than the average amount of compassion. Even though the old woman's haughty behavior was offensive, unattractive, and revealing of a mean nature, the baroness could not bring herself to really despise her.

As she sat drinking her wine and comforting herself with the thought that the old woman, given her age, couldn't be expected to live too much longer, the baroness glanced toward the window and saw a patch of blue in the sky. She got up and looked out. The rain had stopped. Up high, the sun was shining through the clouds.

She decided to have her lunch in the cupola. She rang down to the hotel kitchen with instructions for the maid to bring it to her there. Before starting up the spiral staircase that rose from their living room through the attic to the roof, she refilled her glass and drank it dry, so as not to spill any on the way.

Coming up into the cupola, the baroness felt as if she were mounting to a place at the very top of the world. Tall windows looked out in every direction. She could see the roofs of the houses, the streets, the people walking home from church, and, in the distance, the fields for potatoes and corn, the barracks-like barns of the chicken farms. Fuchsia hung from the ceiling. The leaves of the potted plants on the floor shone big and green in the sun that was coming out. It was like a paradise. Garden chairs were positioned before the windows, each with its own little table on which to set a snack or a drink. A door opened onto the widow's walk where the wife of the sea captain who had built the house once stood behind the iron railing to watch for her husband's sails on the river.

Once there had also been a love seat out there, long ago removed. The baroness remembered its soft velvet cushions and the night when a couple, approaching middle age and content with their life, sat out in the dark hearing the mur-

mur of summer beneath them. In their glasses were summer drinks, gin with soda and slices of lemon. It was on that night the baroness learned that the way the stars helped to make man's fate was by contributing to his certain madness, his search for his own destruction. They were very close on that night, the stars, and so was the moon with its full and terrible light, so that together the stars and the moon made her not quite herself—apparently also having the same effect on her husband, Maxim Maximovich.

It took a little while before she knew she was pregnant. When she knew it, she knew it was from that night on that love seat, on which two people could fit snugly side by side and have a drink of gin. She was forty years old then. She had never been pregnant before. She did not want to be pregnant now, but she was.

It would have been easier on Maxim Maximovich, who was involved at that time in difficult negotiations for the sale of a wood lot that did not have an access or right-of-way to a road, if the baroness simply had stopped speaking to him as other wives did with their husbands when the latter did something wrong.

Rather too late, he had the love seat removed, replacing it with two straight-backed chairs. (The love seat he eventually threw in on the wood lot deal.) This did almost nothing to pacify his wife, who was demanding a resolution and was not going to rest—she was not going to let Maxim Maximovich rest—until one was found.

But what was there to do? She could go to another doctor for a second opinion, but chances were that she would still be pregnant. An abortion? In those days such things were not easy to come by in a small town in Maine, or even in a big one. Perhaps in Boston—although it seemed like a nice city—there were doctors who did not mind breaking the law.

But to find one would mean making inquiries. Where and of whom did one ask such questions? For all the news magazines that he read, which made him by far the most knowledgeable man in town, Maxim Maximovich could come up with no other solution than for his wife to give birth. It was the only way he could think of to make her not pregnant again.

He tried consoling her by recalling the time during their courtship when they had talked idealistically about having a child, possibly two, believing that the more people like themselves the world had, the better off it would be.

This only caused her to remember the frustration of not being able to be a mother when you were ready to be one, not to mention all the wasted effort. Now she was in a worse state—being what you didn't want to be. All she could think of were swollen stomachs. In her dreams they surrounded her, pointing at her like monstrously accusing fingers with bellybuttons on them. She already was of an age when most women were becoming grandmothers, when couples weren't supposed to be carrying on in the way that it was all right for you to carry on when you were young. She thought of the gossip, the snickering. She thought of having to change diapers with poop in them. She started to get hysterical.

By this time, Maxim Maximovich was getting depressed, too. He was thinking of the expense of hiring a baby-sitter every time you wanted to go out. Suppose all the baby-sitters were busy on a given night? They'd be stuck at home, and there was nothing they could do about it. Then just about the time Maxim Maximovich would be getting ready to retire—college. Kids didn't care about the cost, they just wanted to go.

Finally, one day, the baroness thought of something.

"It's God," she said. "I just know it. If it isn't Him, it's one of His saints."

Maxim Maximovich was staring blankly out the window. It was a cold, wet day toward the end of autumn. The trees were bare. The leaves that hadn't been blown away were lying plastered on the sidewalk. Maxim Maximovich's shoulders rose and fell.

"I'm sorry, dear," he said. "Who did you say it possibly is?"

"God," she said. "It could be a saint, although it's hard to know which one. Too bad their ways are so inscrutable—just like the Chinese."

"Well, at least they oppose the Soviets," Maxim Maximovich said. He was looking out at the rain.

"Why shouldn't they?" the baroness said. "The Soviets are a bunch of atheists, after all."

"The Chinese aren't exactly angels," Maxim Maximovich said.

"Why are you talking about the Chinese?" the baroness asked. "I'm talking about God, possibly one of His saints."

"I thought you were talking about the Chinese."

"I'm talking about God," the baroness said. "What I said was, I think it may be some kind of a test. I'm just trying to think it out. This way, it all seems to make sense. You know what I'm talking about. . . ."

"Oh," said Maxim Maximovich. He did not like to talk about what she was talking about.

"It can't be a test for responsibility," the baroness continued. "I think I've already proved that I'm a responsible person. Unless . . ."

"Unless?"

"Unless it's His way of testing for some new kind of leadership position. . . ."

Maxim Maximovich often had thought about running for a district seat in the state legislature. He was smarter than a lot of politicians, already.

He turned from the window and said, "Maybe I'm going to get elected to something."

"I was thinking more in the line of some kind of an honor from the church," the baroness said. "Maybe something from the Metropolitan himself—maybe a place on some kind of national board. No one's done more than I have in the parish. Do you know how much money I've put in the basket already this year?"

"How much?" asked Maxim Maximovich.

"Well, just figure it out. Every single Sunday, two dollars. Every holy day, two more. How much is two times all of that?"

Maxim Maximovich calculated. "It's a lot of money," he said.

"Other people give fifty, seventy-five cents—a dollar at the most. I've seen people who only put in a quarter."

Maxim Maximovich said, "You don't think two dollars is excessive? All right, once in a while . . ."

"That's why I say, maybe it's some kind of an honor."

Although after that Maxim Maximovich got nervous whenever Sundays and holy days came around, he started to feel better about the other situation (they did not like to call the pregnancy by its name). Whenever one of them got depressed or felt somewhat hysterical, the other would start the game of trying to guess what God or one of His saints might have in mind for them. Maybe it was something way beyond public office or an award from the Metropolitan. Maybe they were going to have a child who would be a genius or a famous person! And people one day would nod and say, "No wonder—look who the parents were."

For the present, however, the baroness did not want people knowing anything. As her stomach grew larger, she bought dresses made for ladies who were not pregnant, only fat. When she went visiting, she kept her coat on.

If her host tried to turn up the heat for her, she would say: "Don't bother. The doctor told me, no matter what, don't take off my coat. It's some kind of a bug going around."

At first, people believed it was true. They also began to wear their coats indoors so as not to catch whatever it was that the baroness did not want to get.

Pregnancy was just not a thing they watched for. Long ago they'd tired of speculating why the only couple in town still young enough to do it had not produced an heir. It was one thing for American people not to want to have children: There were too many of them already. But the country was running out of Russians. Who would be left to pray for the return of the Tsar? To remember Stalin's camps? To not forget what happened at Ekaterinburg? To await the day when Holy Russia would fulfill its destiny and save the world?

The ruse with the coat worked only for a little while. When people began getting sick, not from the bug, but from being all bundled up and getting sweaty and then maybe having a draft blowing on them, they knew they had been tricked.

It dawned on them what was going on. They got on their telephones as fast as they could. Former opinions were forced to change. Maybe the baroness couldn't before, but she could now. People counted backwards from the time she began wearing her coat indoors. They figured it happened about the second week of July. Next they set about imagining how it had happened. There was almost no limit to the things some people dreamed up, as old as they were.

As a baby, Sonya was neither fat nor pink nor dimpled,

nor did she laugh when she was tickled. Sometimes she cried so violently she vomited out of her nose. But she was the only Russian child in town—the colony's own little heir—and there was not one of her mother's friends who was not sorely disappointed when the baroness, her mind still set on the church honor, chose as godmother an acquaintance in New York who had a friend who was said to have a connection with someone close to the Metropolitan.

Despite their misgivings, the mother and father even began to feel a little proud. But as Sonya grew, their pride turned to embarrassment. It was bad enough to have a daughter who wanted to be a priest. It was the jumping and the repeating that drove them to their wits' end. It was beyond their imagining what God, or one of His saints, was thinking of. All they knew was that the reward, whatever it was, had better be a good one.

Yet there were happy moments. The baroness tried to think of one as she went out onto the widow's walk and stood at the railing breathing the spring and the winter in the air. In the distance she could see the river winding through the forest, the sun lighting up its surface all the way to the bend. Even the puddles on the sidewalk below were turned to gold. People were coming up the stairs into the hotel for their Sunday dinner. Afterward, they would lie down for their naps or maybe relax before the television. The baroness felt a surge of pride. Why shouldn't she hold up her head? Why shouldn't an old woman show a little respect now and then? She hated to think of all the Russians in the world who did not have a place as good as Plankton to be in. Perhaps someday they would find their way to it. She and Maxim Maximovich already had plans to build an annex on the back.

Suddenly a happy moment came to her. She had known all along that one would. She felt certain that if she only thought for a while longer, she would remember several others. It just was hard to think of them all at once.

This one had occurred on the night of their first party after Sonya's birth, when the baroness no longer had to wear a coat indoors. She remembered she had bought a new dress for the occasion, a black one to make her slim. A number of people remarked on her attractive appearance. From the baby's room, into which they were ushered by the new parents for a peek, the guests had emerged with even more compliments—saying, for instance, that little girls don't come by their looks by chance, they get them from their mothers.

It was a good party in every way. The people ate and drank. No one broke his glass or spilled his plate on the carpet. No one even got very drunk except, perhaps, Maxim Maximovich. At one point in the evening he lay down on the sofa and fell asleep with his drink balanced on his stomach. It made everyone laugh to see it, that little tide of vodka rising and falling with his snores and not a drop spilling. But that was not the happy thing, although it made her laugh.

The happy moment came later, when everyone had gone. Leaving Maxim Maximovich asleep on the sofa, the baroness had poured herself a glass of champagne to take to bed. Passing Sonya's room, she heard a voice inside. It was not a wail or other baby's noise, but an actual voice—as if someone, hearing her going by, had called.

Of course, this was impossible. Sonya at the time was an infant, maybe six months old. She couldn't say anything. Yet when the baroness pushed open the door, there was Sonya in her crib, waiting like a little hostess.

"Naughty girl, are you awake?"

She wasn't talking now. She was lying on her back, her tiny face turned toward the light from the doorway.

"Well, young lady," the baroness said. She went into the room. Under no circumstances was she going to touch the child; the last thing she needed was to feel wet diapers, which at this hour she would have to change herself, or else wake up Maxim Maximovich to do it.

She bent over the crib. Her glass tipped. A little champagne spilled onto her daughter's head.

Sonya jumped. For an instant, she looked as if she were going to cry.

Instead, she began to laugh.

Wiping off the baby's head, the baroness said sillily, "I baptize you in the name of the Mother and the Father and the Holy Champagne."

It may have been sacrilegious, but at the time it seemed very funny. Mother and daughter laughed together. It was the only time the baroness could recall them ever doing that, so that when she thought of it now out on the widow's walk, she thought of it as one of the happy times.

It was only a moment. She never said that it was much.

The baroness held up her glass. The wine shone with the light of the sky. She had a sudden sense of soaring, of being over the center of the world at the very center of time. In the air was the mingling of the seasons. In the wine was the warming sun. She could feel herself loving the town and loving the people and the world and the time the way you love the life that is yours even though it can drive you crazy with worry and be a big responsibility, even a burden, still you can love it.

"I am going to go down to her now," she thought. "She is going to think for certain that she is going to get another

good swat for what she did to me in church and then all the
way home, dragging on my arm like that. I'm going to try
to keep a straight face. And it will be one of the happy times.
We'll go to the river and feed the ducks, she loves to do that,
it will be a good surprise. 'You see, Sonya,' I will say. 'They
are only poor creatures, just as you and I. Look how they
gobble up the bread. Listen to their noise. See how they beat
their wings. Look how they are funny.' And then you will
know that you are not the only one who is. We all are funny,
Sonya. You are only funny in your way.''

But first I am going to finish this, she said to herself,
holding up the bottle. And she poured it and she drank it.

Going down the spiral staircase, she was so excited she
nearly fell.

''I'd better have a drink,'' she thought.

There was some beer left in the refrigerator. She opened
a can. The wine had made her very thirsty. Then she went
down the hall and knocked on Sonya's door. She rapped
hard, so that the child would think that it was something
bad she had done. She called her in the stern way she had
planned—then had to put her hand over her mouth to keep
from laughing and giving it away.

Sonya did not answer.

The baroness opened the door.

Sonya was not there.

The baroness looked in the bathroom. She looked in the
kitchen. She went back to Sonya's room and looked under
the bed.

''If you're hiding . . . ,'' she threatened.

She opened the closet and looked behind the coats.

''Sonya!'' she cried. ''You'd better come out if you know
what's good for you. Do you hear? All right, I'm starting to
get real mad. Sonya! It's a surprise!''

Sonya was running. Sonya was not looking back. The skirt of her pink dress flew out behind her. In a flash she was across the street, ducking between the cars in front of the variety store, then dashing down the alley.

Never before had she left her room without permission. The audacity of it, the freedom of it, made her want to run and run. She cut across a back yard and vaulted a fence. Landing, she saw mud on her shoes and her Sunday dress. She was not afraid. She only marveled that mud could be found at such altitudes.

Now she was up and going fast around a corner, leaning into the curve, making a roaring sound like the motorcycle stunt riders at the fairground. People who heard her looked out their windows. In no time, she roared past the house of the priest and was through the churchyard gate.

And then she stopped. At that moment the sun came from behind a cloud in the patchy sky and struck full at the church. Sonya saw part of the shadow of the entryway break loose and vanish inside.

She looked up and down the street. There was no sign of the farmer's red truck. The churchyard was empty. Sonya closed the gate and locked it with the bolt. She went down the walk and into the church, where the shadow had gone, following it in.

It was a place right for shadows, dark and still as death. A few remaining candles burned before the ikons, their flames sputtering in the wax. All of the sunlight outside was absorbed by the saints on the windows. Their robes flared, their haloes glowed. Tokens of light, dropping through a cracked pane here, a bit of missing glass there, fell onto the floor like small coins.

Sonya stood one step inside. She pulled her long curls across her face to make the beard of a priest.

"I know you're here," she said, sounding only a little afraid.

She took another step in.

"I've run away. We can go away together now. Forever, if you'd like."

She was saying this aloud, not in the soundless way in which they always had spoken before. The time had come for saying things out.

"Are the children with you?" She stretched her neck, looking into the dark. "Olga . . . Marie . . . Anastasia? You can come out. It's me. . . ."

There was no movement, no sound from anywhere. Sonya closed her eyes. It took a long time, but eventually they came out, one by one: in their long dresses, in their sailor suits, in their crowns.

But as usual when they appeared, the old woman was not there.

"It's because she's one of you, isn't she?" Sonya said. She was advancing now into the dark, less and less afraid.

"That's why you always disappear," she said, looking for the right shadow. "Why you only light six candles, even though there were seven of you. Why you kiss all the dead people good-bye. You think it's your obligation. I'm right, aren't I? Only, which one of you is she? There's no need to keep it a secret any longer. Don't you hear? I'm the only one who's going to be left. I'm the one you have to tell."

It was long past the dinner hour when Sonya came home. Her mother was suffering from a bad headache. She was extremely angry.

"And here I was, ready to give you a surprise," she said. "What do you mean, running off like that?"

Sonya did not need to be told to go to her room.

She looked at her mother and father and in a calm, steady voice said: "I hope you don't mind, but I've invited her home. She'll be coming here from now on. I've decided that." And she went into her room and closed the door.

"What was that all about?" asked Maxim Maximovich. He was home from selling houses. He had his shoes off and his feet up on the hassock. He was reading the Sunday newspaper and having a drink.

"I can't take this anymore," said his wife.

"Now don't be getting yourself upset," Maxim Maximovich said. "I'll go and see." He got up and went to Sonya's door. He could hear her inside, talking to herself.

"Don't worry, you're safe with me," she was saying, not repeating, saying it quietly, saying it not exaggeratedly as in play but as if someone were actually in the room with her.

Maxim Maximovich bent to the keyhole.

"When you want to, just tell me, and we'll go away," Sonya was saying. "Wherever you want, that's where we'll go. The summer place, or the winter. If there's a place for spring, we'll go there, too. You decide."

Maxim Maximovich looked, but he couldn't see a soul.

the
last
song
of
exile

1

The day he quit his job scrubbing pots in the kitchen of the
Hotel Nicholas the Second, Gregor Mironovich Smolnov an-
nounced to his wife that they were moving to Austria, where
he had been a Displaced Person after the Second World War.
Gregor Mironovich remembered the mountains, the swept
streets, bakeries that made bread with a thick crust, the cool
air in the orchard where he had worked. He remembered

that for a few schillings a week you could have a room with a view of the mountains and with flowers in the window. His wife, Lisaveta Stepanova, had never been to Austria, her own path to America having led through Harbin and Shanghai. She imagined a little apartment that she would keep fresh and clean, a bed with big plump pillows, a breakfast nook by the window where the flowers were. From the window they would be able to look out at the river Grisha had talked about, the one that came down from the mountains, flowing like milk under the bridges of the town.

A person can never know for certain the ground in which his bones will lie, or the language in which one's final prayer will be uttered; yet Lisaveta Stepanova would not have believed that another journey in her life was possible. She was nearly seventy, and she was tired. She had come to accept their small room over the hotel kitchen as her last stop in life. She tried to keep the room nice with a clean tablecloth on the table and, before the ikon, a candle. On Sunday, when she had a little time off, she picked wildflowers in the pasture behind the post office and put them on the window sill. The room looked out on the alley and not much sunlight came in. But there was a door that locked securely behind you and a roof that kept off the rain. On their hot plate she was able to make a pot of tea or a bowl of soup. Gregor Mironovich was allowed to park their old car in the hotel lot free of charge. Their television was right at the foot of the bed. At night they propped up their pillows and watched it until they fell asleep.

When her husband's job came to its sudden end, Lisaveta Stepanova was afraid they would be evicted. The baroness, who owned the hotel, had caught him in the storage room with a bottle of vodka apparently pilfered from the bar. This was not long after his friend, Victor Shostakovich, had died in a room upstairs one night, so Gregor Mironovich was feeling depressed.

A terrible argument had ensued. During it, the baroness said he was fired. Gregor Mironovich, in protest, quit. The next day the baroness summoned Lisaveta Stepanova to her office. She said that she had decided they could keep their room. Lisaveta Stepanova was humble with gratitude. The baroness said that Lisaveta Stepanova, who cleaned, waited on tables, worked as her maid, and helped out the hotel cook, should not be made to suffer just because she was married to Gregor Mironovich, which, the baroness said, must be suffering enough.

The baroness laid down a rule that Gregor Mironovich was not to come near the kitchen again. He had called her names, she said, which she had not deserved after giving him steady employment all these years. Now their rent was deducted from one pay check instead of from two. Lisaveta Stepanova continued to take her meals in the kitchen, which helped financially. Once in a while when the baroness was away, Ivanov the cook prepared a plate for her to take upstairs to Gregor Mironovich. In his pride, he refused to eat it, unless it was something good.

Gregor Mironovich passed the first weeks of his retirement preparing for their return to Austria. From the library he borrowed books with maps that folded out and almanacs that gave the populations of the countries of the world and listed their main crops and mineral deposits. He wrote for travel guides from the American Automobile Association. Every few days he telephoned the tourist office in Augusta to see if the air fare to Vienna had gone up or down, then took out their bank book and calculated how much money would be left to live on. He sent off letters to two or three old acquaintances in Austria whom he believed to be still alive, carefully writing on the envelopes the names of their towns and the streets on which they lived, as far as he could remember them. Of each he enquired about rents in their neighborhoods, and wondered if he might stay with them a few days until he could find a place. As he waited for their replies, he began to sell off belongings that would not fit into a suitcase—the phonograph, the coat rack, the quilt from their bed, the electric space heater. When he met someone on the street and that person, in parting, said, "See you again, Gregor Mironovich," Gregor Mironovich would smile and say, "Maybe."

In the afternoon when he was done with his day's planning, Gregor Mironovich took his fishing pole and walked down to the river. Turning over a rock, he found a worm for his hook. The sunshine came through the leaves, the birds sang, the flies buzzed lazily near his ears. He sat on a rock warmed by the sun and cast his line into the water. A breeze just strong enough to blow away the gnats floated petals from a cherry tree down upon his shoulders.

Some afternoons he would meet on the river bank Father Vladimir, the old priest from the Holy Virgin of Kazan. Father Vladimir believed there were sturgeon in the river and it was his plan to catch one and to sell the roe and make the town rich. He had bought a lot of nylon string and tied it into a net which he stretched across the narrow part of the river. So far no sturgeon had swum into it.

"Somehow, they're getting through." The old priest wore a puzzled expression as he looked out over the river. "They must have found a passage underneath. Well, you can't blame them for not wanting to get caught. God gave them a life to keep for as long as they can, just as He did for us."

Gregor Mironovich watched what he said around Father Vladimir. His church was under the jurisdiction of the Russian Orthodox Church of America, which recognized the legitimacy of the patriarch in Moscow. This caused some people in town to say that Father Vladimir was a Soviet agent, sent to Plankton to find out what he could.

"Do you think the baroness could use some caviar up at the hotel?" the priest wondered. "I'm trying to line up as many customers as I can."

"In Austria," said Gregor Mironovich, being careful, "you can catch fish as big as your arm."

"That's very big," said Father Vladimir.

"You don't have to be afraid to eat them, either," Gregor Mironovich said. "Over there the water's clean, not like here."

One day Gregor Mironovich found sitting on his fishing rock a young man with a beard. It was Christian, the American who had learned in college how to play the balalaika. People said he moved to the town because he liked Russians so much.

"Good day!" he said with a smile as Gregor Mironovich came down the path from the road.

He looked at Christian and at the rock on which he sat. On the young man's lap was a pad of music paper. He appeared to be writing a song. Gregor Mironovich set down his fishing pole and his can of dirt for the worms. The hook dangled close to the intruder's ear but he did not seem to know enough to go somewhere else.

Gregor Mironovich decided to give him a chance to move while he looked for worms. Under one rock was a worm but it was very quick and it got down into its hole before he could grab it. The worm under the next rock he got only a tiny piece of. He found a log and tried to roll it over. It was stuck in the wet ground.

Christian rose from the fishing rock. "I'll help you," he said.

"Don't need it help," said Gregor Mironovich, his face red from the strain.

The young man got his fingers down into the mud and lifted. The log went over. Underneath were some nice fat worms.

Christian held the can while Gregor Mironovich put them in. They were big ones, the kind you usually only can catch at night with a flashlight.

"They're beauties," said Christian.

"I know how to find good ones," said Gregor Mironovich. He took one and threaded it onto his hook. "I usually sit on that stone," he said. "But you can use it today, if you want."

"I don't want to take your rock," said Christian. "You should have told me."

"You don't have to move. I can find somewhere else to sit."

"No, it's your place. Look, this is fine here." Christian took his music to a tree next to the water. The roots came out and made a little lap for him to sit on.

"Are you certain?" said Gregor Mironovich. "Because I can sit somewhere else."

"It's perfect, really."

"It looks like a good place. Is that music you're writing?"

"Yes, it's a song. This, I can do anywhere. For fishing, you need the right place."

In this way they became friends. All during that summer,

while Gregor Mironovich waited for a letter from Austria, they met on the bank of the river on days when the weather was fine. Christian was a teacher. In the summer when school closed he did not look for another job because he liked to work on his songs. Sometimes he brought along a book to read but mostly he brought his music. On occasion he brought his balalaika. Sitting on the lap of the tree, he wrote notes onto the paper and then he played them.

One day Father Vladimir, who came down to check his net, asked, "What kind of a song is that? It sounds sad."

"It's a Russian song," Christian said.

"Song for crying," said Gregor Mironovich. From time to time he liked to tease or make a little joke.

"It's going to be a love song."

"But love isn't sad," said the priest.

"Worse than sad," said Gregor Mironovich. "From start to finish, big headache, big tragedy. Better to fish, and forget about it."

"People die, people go away," Christian said. "People don't always love you back."

"I remember when my wife died," Father Vladimir said. "It was a great sadness for me. Of course, it was only because I had been so happy. The world goes around, and we go around with it. Everything happens to us twice, once as joy, once as pain."

"I'm thinking it would be nice to have Russian words for the song," Christian said. "Maybe you can help me."

"I can try," said Father Vladimir. He was squatting near the water, tapping circles onto its surface with a stick.

"First I have to get the music right," said Christian. "I want the music to tell about the sadness before the words. I'm not sure yet that I can do it, to make it the way I want it to be. Anyhow, it's not entirely sad. Maybe I don't even know yet what the feeling is."

Toward the middle of summer it rained for several days in a row. Gregor Mironovich stayed home studying his maps, underlining the names of the cities and towns where it might be nice to live. In the afternoon he turned on the soap operas on the television. He pulled his chair over to the window and watched the rain making puddles in the alley. He took long naps.

On Friday of the rainy week, Christian came to the hotel. He found his way to the room over the kitchen and knocked on the door.

Gregor Mironovich was not used to visitors. He opened the door a crack to see who it was.

"Elaine and I want you to come out for dinner," Christian said.

In all the years they had lived in the hotel, no one had ever invited them to dinner, unless it was to a funeral meal when everybody who showed up at the church could come.

"Not possible," said Gregor Mironovich. Soon he would be in Austria. He didn't need invitations now.

"We can pick you up, if that's a problem."

Gregor Mironovich did not say anything. He opened the door and wiggled his finger for Christian to follow him. He led him to the window.

"You see?" he said.

Christian looked across the alley at the wall of the market next door. He nodded to Gregor Mironovich. He did not know what he was supposed to be seeing, or even why he was nodding.

"You think I don't have a car?" asked Gregor Mironovich. "Go ahead, look. You see this alley? It goes to the back. That's where the parking lot is. That's where I keep my car."

He looked down the alley in the direction in which Christian was supposed to look. "You can't see it from here. Some day I show you."

"I drew a map," Christian said, taking a piece of paper from his shirt pocket. "We're thinking about Sunday. Is that all right? It wouldn't be until afternoon. I know your wife goes to church."

Gregor Mironovich shook his head. "My wife is too tired."

"It will be good for her, then."

They lived in a farmhouse whose fields were overgrown with bushes and trees. Christian had bought the place thinking to become an organic farmer, refraining from using insecticides and factory-made fertilizers in order to give better health to the people who would buy his vegetables. He felt there was a big market for this. But after spading up a plot of clayish earth just big enough to grow a few stalks of corn, which the raccoons ate, and enough tomatoes for one winter's worth of spaghetti sauce, he decided to return to teaching.

They continued, however, to keep two goats and some chickens. The goats lived in a shed attached to the house. Out back, Christian fenced in a yard for the chickens. In the morning he liked to go out and feel under the hens for eggs. He also bought a goose, which he intended to kill for Christmas. But when the time came, he could not do it. Even when he dug in his garden he was always afraid of his spade dissecting a toad under the soil.

The goose honked loudly at Gregor Mironovich and Lisaveta Stepanova as they walked from their car to the kitchen door. It seemed to be trumpeting the fact that it was still alive. The goats came to the window of their shed and peered out with their pale rakish eyes.

The house on the inside looked to Gregor Mironovich as

if it had been built by a shoemaker, not a carpenter. The ceiling plaster was cracked, the floor sloped, the wallpaper was put on crooked, more paint was on the window glass than on the frames. In every corner and on every shelf were books and phonograph records—too many of them, in Gregor Mironovich's opinion.

"I apologize for the mess," Christian's wife said. She was a young woman with long black hair and she wore glasses. "If we waited until the place was neat, we'd never have anybody."

Once by the river, Gregor Mironovich had asked his new friend if it were true what people said, that his wife was a Jew. He tried to be subtle.

"I was wondering, do you go to the synagogue with your wife?"

He remembered how Christian had smiled.

"We're part of a long line of Christians," he said, which Gregor Mironovich later realized was probably a play on words.

They sat at the table. None of the plates matched. The meat was brought in a pot that did not look very clean. Christian filled their glasses with wine. There was only one kind, red. For dessert they ate strawberries. The cream came to the rim of their bowls, all of which were chipped.

In another room a baby cried. Christian's wife excused herself. For a little while Christian played the balalaika to entertain his guests. Lisaveta Stepanova tapped her fingers in time on her lap.

Elaine came in with the child and said, "Would you like to hold her? Her name's Becky."

"Oh, yes," said Lisaveta Stepanova.

She rocked the baby in her arms. She looked adoringly into its small face and spoke to it with soft Russian words.

Gregor Mironovich grew impatient and went to the window and looked out at the gray sky. Christian brought over his glass of wine. "I'm glad to have you for a friend," he said.

When it was time to go, the young woman kissed Gregor Mironovich on his cheek. They had only just met, yet she did this.

The next day the weather cleared. When Gregor Mironovich arrived at the river, Christian was waiting. On his knees was his music, on his face his smile.

On Gregor Mironovich's fishing rock was a box of dirt. It was filled with worms.

"I dug them from our garden," Christian said.

The sun made the river sparkle. The trees, the rocks, the earth were filled with a good smell after the long rain. Gregor Mironovich caught four sunfish and an eel. But he was not glad. There still had been no reply from Austria. And now there was something else. This troubling new thing, a friendship.

Lisaveta Stepanova invited the young couple to their room the following Sunday. She apologized for not being able to cook a proper meal on the hot plate. They said not to worry about it, but she did. The next time they came, she rose very early, before anyone was up, and prepared their meal in the hotel kitchen, getting it ready then going to church and coming back and finishing it off and carrying it upstairs. The Americans said it was the finest food they had ever eaten. Gregor Mironovich watched as his wife, drunk on their compliments, invited them back.

Each time they brought a gift. One time it was tomatoes. Another time it was bread they had baked themselves. As summer ended, Elaine began to knit a vest. She finished it at their table after dinner. She made Gregor Mironovich stand and try it on.

Finally one afternoon when he returned from the river, Gregor Mironovich found in his mailbox a letter with large colorful stamps. He became so excited he had a hard time getting his key into the lock. Once inside, he got out his eyeglasses and studied the return address. The town he recognized but not the name of the sender. Carefully he slit the envelope with a knife.

The letter was written in bad Russian, with many misspellings.

Dear Mr. Smolnov,

Excuse, please, that I do not write so well in Russian but it is a language I seldom speak and never write, although my parents taught me. I am married for 12 years to a Hungarian, a refugee like you and Papa, only from 1956, when they made their revolution in Budapest. At least Hungary is close and there are many other what they call Freedom Fighter here, so my husband is not losing almost his mother tongue as I am in sending you the sad news that Papa is dead for several years. In luck, the postman remembered him and brought your letter. Mother also is dead. I have four children by this Hungarian. They only know to speak German, which is our language now, although I try to teach a few words Russian. You imagine life here is good but let me tell you it is your dream only. What you think is price for a room is price not even for a cup of coffee and piece of cake. My husband is without work for almost a year. The factory is not hiring anymore. If you want an apartment, you must wait on a long list. My advice is to stay in America. Know when you have good fortune. My husband has uncle in Cleveland Ohio. We wrote to him also, maybe he knows of some work we can have there. So far we heard nothing.

> With respectful greetings,
> Mrs. Imre (Luba) Lengyel

He was sitting at his table on which his maps were spread. Very slowly he put down the letter. Very slowly he closed his eyes.

2

They moved out of the hotel into a little house in the woods. The house was bought with their passage money. It was far from the town, far from the river—far from Austria—on a dirt road, a couple of miles in from the highway. Gregor Mironovich bought it in the fall, just after he received the letter from Mrs. Lengyel. The man who sold it said all it needed was some paint and a few shingles where the rain leaked through, a bit of tidying up.

"There's quiet out here, that's the main thing." The man had a large red face. His stomach hung over his belt like a sack of flour. He showed Gregor Mironovich through the four rooms of the house and then took him outside.

"Listen," he said. "Do you hear it?"

Gregor Mironovich listened.

"That's the quiet. There's nobody going to come way out here to trouble a person."

Any time you wanted, he said, you could shoot yourself a deer or a moose. It didn't matter the season, the woods were full of them. Now and then you still came across the track of a bear. And there were coyotes. You should kill as many of these as you could. They were raising havoc with the deer herd, he said, running down a lot of deer that otherwise hunters might have been able to shoot. He had used the house mainly for a hunting camp. Or sometimes he would just come out with a few friends for a game of cards. He led Gregor Mironovich around the patch of yard. The gully at the edge of the woods was filled with beer cans.

"You don't have to be bothered with mowing a lot of grass," the man said. "That's why I kept the yard on the small side. And these here gas tanks are for the stove that goes with the house. I'm throwing them in, free of charge. And look over there. You even got a flagpole."

All their belongings that Gregor Mironovich had not sold they managed to load into the back seat and trunk of the car or tie onto the roof. Ivanov the cook helped them carry the mattress and bed frame down the stairs. He shook their hands outside the back door and returned to his kitchen to start working on lunch. As they drove away, they looked back for someone to wave good-bye to, but no one was paying any attention. Two of the hotel's elderly residents were on the front porch, leaning forward on their canes, talking close to each other's ear. Lisaveta Stepanova waved but they didn't see her.

It took Christian two weeks to locate them.

"Why didn't you tell us?" he asked on the telephone. "We could have helped you."

"Everything is happening so quickly," Lisaveta Stepanova said. "We don't like to bother you."

She made the occasion of their first visit a party. She cooked up a huge pot of borscht. From the store on the highway she bought a bottle of wine and a half gallon of ice cream. She had asked Christian to bring his balalaika. After dinner he played it. Gregor Mironovich went into the next room to watch television. He was in a mood; Lisaveta Stepanova wasn't sure what kind.

"Do you recognize this one?" Christian asked, leaning forward in his chair to look at Gregor Mironovich through the doorway. "It's our song from the river. I've changed it somewhat."

Gregor Mironovich shrugged. "Sounds like before."

"Not all of it. Listen." He had put a soft lilt into one part of it, a few notes up high near the bridge, not enough so that you would say it was a happy song, although now it was not entirely sad.

"Same thing," said Gregor Mironovich. He turned back to his television.

"I think he's not feeling good," Lisaveta Stepanova said in a lowered voice a little later. "He feels badly that his plan about Austria didn't come out. He told too many people about it, and now he's ashamed."

That winter Gregor Mironovich had his three-hundred-dollar accident.

It was snowing. Gregor Mironovich was driving with his wife to the cash market out on the highway to buy some groceries for Sunday dinner. He was turning left across the road into the parking lot when a car came along from the other direction and skidded into his fender.

When the state trooper arrived to investigate, the other driver, a young man, got into the police car. Gregor Mironovich observed them talking together for a long time. He and Lisaveta Stepanova wrapped themselves in the seat blanket and waited. Finally the trooper, a tall man with red sideburns, came over with a clipboard.

Gregor Mironovich told the policeman the young lunatic was speeding.

"Half your car's still in the road," the policeman said. This was not the truth, for a good deal more than half was in the parking lot.

"He says a pickup truck was in front of you," the trooper said. He pointed with his long chin in the direction of the other driver, who was still in the police car. "He figures you couldn't see him coming because of the truck blocking your view."

The American glasses Gregor Mironovich wore did not permit him always to see great distances, but there was nothing wrong with the eyes of Lisaveta Stepanova, who ordinarily warned him of obstacles in the road.

She had not mentioned a truck.

"Is a lie," he said.

The policeman looked at Gregor Mironovich's license. Gregor Mironovich waited nervously while he filled out a report. The policeman handed back his license and gave him a slip of paper with the other driver's name and address. He said they both should get in touch with their insurance companies.

When he realized that the policeman meant to let the lunatic go free, Gregor Mironovich jumped from his car and ran around to his dented fender.

"Who pay?" he shouted. "Who pay?" Lisaveta Stepanova rolled down the window and pleaded with him not to excite himself.

The trooper walked away. It was then Gregor Mironovich noticed that the policeman's right leg bowed out.

The next day, Christian and Elaine came to visit, as was their custom now on Sundays.

Lisaveta Stepanova, who knew more American words, told the story. Gregor Mironovich drew a diagram. He said it was a lie about the truck, he had seen them whispering, and the policeman's leg, the right one, had swung out.

Leaning close over the table, he lowered his voice.

"Jewish," he said, whispering to give it meaning.

He saw how they looked at one another.

"Jewish man," he said a little impatiently, like a teacher having to go over elementary facts with his pupils, "is walking always with right leg coming out."

They waited for him to go on but he did not know the word in English. He moved two fingers like a scissors and tried to imitate a snipping noise but they did not seem to comprehend. At last he explained it in Russian to Lisaveta Stepanova.

"Grisha is saying," the old woman began, looking embarrassed, "that always the right leg of Jewish man is bending out because . . . because of what they are doing to Jewish boys . . . down there . . . on their little things. Grisha is saying this is making them very sore. So they are learning already as little boy to swing out their leg so it's not rubbing."

The Americans responded with a laugh. Apparently, they thought it was funny. Then to Gregor Mironovich's amazement, Christian confessed that he himself was this American word—*circumcised*. He said that he did not walk with his right leg swinging out; but when he walked away from the table to show them, it did.

"Is hard for you to see," Gregor Mironovich smiled triumphantly.

The insurance company, going by Gregor Mironovich's own diagram, found him to be at fault. He did not have insurance for collisions. He did not have the three hundred dollars the man at the garage said it would cost to fix his fender.

Somewhere in the accident report they had helped him to fill out, the two Americans, he realized finally, must have put the blame on him.

He came to realize this on a Saturday morning as he was watching the *Laurel and Hardy Funtime Feature* on Channel 8, one of his favorite shows. He was in his armchair, not more than a few feet from the television, so he could not have been mistaken, as his wife claimed.

Every few minutes, the program was interrupted by advertising. It was election time. Besides selling candy bars, computers, and sandwiches that had names like performers in a circus—Big Max, Chicken McNougat—they were selling politicians: sheriffs, county commissioners, senators, and other kinds.

Gregor Mironovich tried not to watch. He did not want to encourage them. Long ago he had come to the conclusion that the purpose of America—he suspected it was in the Constitution, somewhere in the small print—was to make money. Not just a little money, with which people in Austria and other parts of the world might be content, but much money. Once one aspirin was good enough for a headache; now they said take two. To Gregor Mironovich, it was a ploy by the Bayer Aspirin Company to double its sales. The Alka-Seltzer Company also was doing it.

He looked up at the ceiling, glanced through the *TV Guide*, plucked at the stuffing coming through the arm of his chair. All the while he emitted sighs of impatience and disgust, trying not to watch.

Then he heard the name.

He looked. It was there before his eyes: WRIGHT.

It was the name of the lunatic!

The television showed the picture of a man—not the lunatic, but the resemblance was strong. A voice was exhorting people to vote for him. Then, in a rapid undertone, as if trying to hide something, the voice said, "Paid for by Citizens for Wright; Howard Shapiro, treasurer."

When Lisaveta Stepanova looked in from the kitchen to say that lunch was ready, she found Gregor Mironovich sitting as if in a trance, his small shiny fingers clutching the arms of the chair. Behind his spotted glasses his eyes were huge.

"Grisha?" she said apprehensively.

Gregor Mironovich jumped to his feet, pointing a finger at the television as if, by a slip of the tongue, it had incriminated itself.

"Wright!" he said.

At last he understood. It was for political gain that Christian and his wife had decided to betray him. They hoped to curry favor with the politician Wright by exculpating, in the accident report, his son or other close relative, the lunatic. And in the background was a man named Shapiro who—they said it right on the television—had a treasure; not to mention the policeman who had walked with his right leg swinging out as, curiously, had Christian's.

At first Lisaveta Stepanova laughed, just like the two Americans. Then she began to argue. At one point she accused him of having a brain sickness—a cancer she called it—from the time of the camp.

She tried to run away, but he pursued her everywhere. By the time they were in bed, she was pleading with him to stop. Finally—it must have been very late, sometime after midnight—he got her to admit at least that it was possible.

Lisaveta Stepanova was quiet for a long time.

Gregor Mironovich turned in the bed to look at her, but the night had neither stars nor moon to shine in his window and he could not tell if the dark silent shape curled into a ball beside him, its toenails positioned like spikes to keep him away, was asleep or only pretending.

He rose on his elbow.

"Lisaveta," he said.

Her breath blew with a bad smell in his face.

Gregor Mironovich lay back and sighed. He started to feel sleepy. He closed his eyes. But just as he dozed off, he was awakened by the racing of the mice in the ceiling. They were also running up and down behind the walls. It was November. Winter was at hand. There was a frenzy in the way they ran, as if they were desperate to get in.

His eyes followed the sound of their scampering feet over his head. He remembered the vest Elaine had knitted for him, the worms Christian had dug. It was then, he supposed, that he first knew that they were up to something. So he had never really been fooled. Maybe at times, when he had relaxed his guard, he had been a little deceived. But never really fooled.

He was older than Lisaveta Stepanova. He would be the first to die. She was a simple, trusting soul who believed them to be genuinely kind and called them "children," as if they were her own. The disarming of a lonely old woman inexperienced in conspiracies had been at the center of their plan all along. It had been through her, he remembered, that they had talked him into applying for a property tax refund for people who were old. Naturally, they then had volunteered—as they had with the accident report—to help fill out papers that required him to state exactly his financial worth. Once he was gone, it would all fall into their hands: television, new kitchen table, a car that was still in good running condition despite its three-hundred-dollar dent . . . even the bed in which he lay. Also the house was worth a lot more since Christian had helped him patch the roof and jack up the corner where it sagged.

Gregor Mironovich thanked God for giving him a mind

capable of sorting out good from evil. He decided that the next time he gave her a ride into the town to go to church, he would have Lisaveta Stepanova light a candle before the ikon of the Virgin of Kazan as a way of giving thanks for the *Laurel and Hardy Funtime Feature* on Channel 8.

Suddenly, Gregor Mironovich jumped in his bed. A wild racing rumbled across the ceiling and down the wall just behind his head.

These were not mice.

"What's wrong? What is it?" The old woman's voice came quick in the dark.

"Rats!" he said. He had seen one just that morning eating seeds under the bird feeder outside the kitchen window.

"Please, Grisha. Don't talk that way anymore."

"Grisha, what? All you want to do is argue. Go to sleep. I'll take care of them tomorrow. I have my gun."

"Grisha! Are you crazy?"

"You're the one who's crazy. Go to sleep, old woman. It's almost morning."

He lay down but he did not sleep, not for a long time, not until the night began to lighten in his window.

3

She had not answered when he said her name because she could not bear to hear him speak more of it. The more he spoke of it, the more his awful suspicion hardened in him, like cement. And she knew that once it had set it would be there forever with its ponderous weight.

She did not believe they had betrayed him, but when she said this, he had shouted at her with much anger, his face turning the color of a bruise. Her resistance had cracked the way the limbs of the willow in their dooryard cracked and fell when the wind blew hard in winter. The morning would bring another Sunday. They would come to visit. He would accuse them. And when they turned to her because they knew well how he was apt to be, she would concede that it was possible. And then they would never come again.

A person could not bargain with God for his fate. Sometimes fortune hanged you by the neck, other times it led you to the river to drown. Her it had brought to a shack in a clearing in the woods in America to spend the last of her days with an old man going mad.

She had never loved him, but she had been a widow, her hair already gray, when he came to work in the hotel and she did not want to live the rest of her life alone. She was making up the room that was to be his, and when she looked he was standing in the doorway with his suspicious eyes. He had no hair, his few teeth were yellow, his suit fit so poorly it looked as if, at any sudden movement, it might drop off.

On Sunday sometimes they walked to the river and sat in the grass. She was careful not to ask too much in the beginning. Eventually, bit by bit, he told her everything. His father, his mother, his grandfather, his grandmother, his brothers, his sisters—all of them shot. He had been far away, cutting trees in the forest. Later, for telling a friend a joke about Stalin, they arrested his wife and shot her and took away his daughter. This was after he himself had been arrested, and beaten, and put in the camp.

Now he had a mouth full of large uniform teeth that clicked when he talked. Only now her pity for him was surpassed by her sorrow for herself.

One night after they were married she swallowed many

pills but not enough. She woke in a hospital. She heard voices outside the door. Then he entered and sat in a chair. He did not know she was awake. When she looked at him, he had his face in his hands. Tears were coming through his fingers.

Now in his morning sleep, with the gray light of the gray dawn in the window, his fingers twitched, contracted, tried to close a grip. His feet kicked under the blanket, chasing or being chased. Under his lids, his eyes darted back and forth like a lizard's. His mouth was a black hole into which something might have sunk. From the water glass on the bedstand his even white teeth leered at Lisaveta Stepanova as if from the devilment of his dream.

She rose wearily, her eyes ringed with the color of her sleepless night. Her hands lingered at each button of her dress, holding onto the cloth as if they lacked the strength to go on. Slowly she made her way down the stairs. There was a sour taste in her mouth, a fire smouldered in her stomach, and when she went to the toilet her urine burned. Her face in the mirror was as white as her hair.

"Am I already dead?" she wondered.

When his coffee was ready she called but he did not answer. She heated a cup of milk for her stomach and stared with an empty look through the sheet of plastic tacked over the kitchen window to keep out the draft. The plastic made a blur of the bird feeder, the naked willow with its broken limbs, the trees at the edge of the brown grass, the flagpole in their yard which did not have a flag, only a piece of rope hanging down its side.

This must be the way he sees all things, she thought. All around him were indistinct shapes and images that he distrusted and feared because he could not be certain what they were. It was a kind of cataract that had descended over not just his eyes but his heart.

She remembered the time Christian had asked why they did not have a flag for the pole. That had started Gregor Mironovich on a mighty recitation of America's many faults, among the worst of which were doctors, banks, lawyers, middlemen who sold vegetables to the grocery stores, union presidents, garage mechanics, the big pill companies, the newspapers, and all the politicians.

It was not the first time they had heard this, but this time Christian, who had been his friend, said, "Well, I'm an American and I don't cheat and I don't steal and I try not to lie and I don't think I take advantage of anyone."

"That," Gregor Mironovich had declared majestically, "is because you are like a Russian."

They could have stayed in the hotel; they could have taken other rooms in the town. One afternoon she had come up from the kitchen and on the table found the letter from Austria and their bank book with all their savings—seven thousand dollars—withdrawn. The next thing she knew they were living in the woods, miles from anywhere. The house had stood empty for years, you could tell from the smell of it. The floor heaved with the frost, the wind blew through the windows and doors, the rain made brown stains on the ceiling and wallpaper. They never went back, except for church on Easter. Gregor Mironovich said he did not want to set his foot into a town where he had had to wash pots and peel onions when he could have been a manager in any place where hotels were not permitted to discriminate because of age or a person not being born of a high family as some people pretended to be.

Lisaveta Stepanova's empty gaze drifted into the living

174

room, a room as gray and as bleak as the day. In its holder, the ikon candle burned low, its flame about to be extinguished in its wax. The television and Gregor Mironovich's armchair faced each other in gloomy silence, like two old people with nothing left to say. Gregor Mironovich's twenty-two rifle was in the corner. When she saw it her hand shook so that the milk spilled out of the cup onto her dress.

She did not even bother to wipe the milk off, her eyes were frozen on the gun. She stood and crossed the room quickly, then slowing the last few steps, approached cautiously, as if the gun were a snake.

She grasped it that way, by its sleek black neck, the way you would grasp a snake behind the head so it cannot turn and bite. Looking for a place to hide it, she carried it off to the kitchen, then into the pantry. There she laid it on the floor, behind the sack of sunflower seeds she kept for the birds and squirrels. If it was not concealed, neither was it conspicuous. If Gregor Mironovich said anything, she would simply say she had not hidden it, only moved it to a new place, out of the way, the room in which you keep your ikon not being the proper place for a gun.

She was fixing dinner when the ceiling groaned over her head. In a little while Gregor Mironovich came down and sat at the kitchen table. She kept her back to him. He began to whistle in his irritating way, a whistle without a melody, more wind than song. He kept it up and kept it up until she could not stand it. She fled into the bathroom. She leaned against the door as if she had gained sanctuary from a mob. Presently she heard him moving about. Then the room was still. She put her ear to the door. On the other side she heard his wheezy breath.

"I am going out," he said. But he did not go. She could

feel his presence through the door. He was listening, waiting. She did not say a word. At last he moved away. She heard the front door. When she looked out she saw his figure, old and vague, pass slowly in front of the kitchen window.

Christian and his wife arrived at noon. They sat at the kitchen table. Elaine took from her bag a handful of russet-colored yarn, which she was knitting into a winter hat for Gregor Mironovich. It had long ear flaps to tie under the chin.

"Where's Gregor?" Christian asked. "I have incredible news for him," he said excitedly. "Can you believe it? Father Vladimir caught a sturgeon! At least he thinks it's a sturgeon. . . . It's very big."

But Lisaveta Stepanova was not listening. She looked nervously out the window. Nowhere did she see a blur resembling Gregor Mironovich.

"I don't know," she said. "I don't see him." She tried to sound not worried, but annoyed. "Never mind. We can start without him."

"It was a huge one," Christian said. "And it swam into his net. It was so big, he ran to town for help. They say he came into the hotel shouting, 'We're saved, we're saved!' At first, people thought there had been a coup in Moscow. It took four men to haul the fish out of the water."

She could see he was talking, but her ears were deafened with the pounding of the blood from her heart. She moved mechanically between the stove and the table, bringing the food.

For Gregor Mironovich not to come in, she thought, would be the greatest of insults to people who were, after all, guests. But to come in and accuse your guests, to call them traitors, even threaten to get a gun as he had in bed that very morning . . .

When she thought of the gun, her breath stopped short. She went to the pantry. The rifle was gone. She ran into the living room. It was not in its old place near the ikon. It was not anywhere.

The Americans, their cheeks round with food, regarded her curiously.

Something out the window caught Lisaveta Stepanova's eye. She squinted at the place in the distance by the willow where something had moved and now was still.

She heard the puck through the glass and plastic sheet. She did not know at first that it was the sound of a bullet. Looking down, she saw the cleft in Christian's ear. It made her think of a tiny cave in a cliff face, the sun on its floor. Then a dark red droplet welled into it. Christian put his hand up and the blood came through his fingers. His wife uttered a small cry and began searching in her purse.

The rifle fired again. The windowpane shattered.

"God help us!" gasped Lisaveta Stepanova. "He wants to kill us all!"

In a single movement the three of them were under the table.

Unable to find a hanky in her purse, Elaine grabbed Gregor Mironovich's russet-colored winter hat with the long ear flaps and tied it around her husband's head. His head was shaking as if it were on a spring.

"It's Grisha!" wailed the old woman. "He called you rats!"

The younger woman began to scream for help.

"Hush!" Lisaveta Stepanova said. They were on their hands and knees, their faces close together under the table, their back ends butting out from under the tablecloth.

They heard whistling.

"My God, he's coming!" Elaine said.

"Quickly," Lisaveta Stepanova pushed Christian by the shoulder. "Lock the door. I'm calling the police."

"I'm wounded," Christian said.

"Please," said Lisaveta Stepanova. "Before he is coming."

Raising the ear flap of Gregor Mironovich's russet-colored winter hat from over his eyes, Christian stuck his head out from under the table. On his hands and knees he scrambled to the front door, the russet-colored yarn, playing out from his wife's knitting bag, following him like the thread of a gigantic spider.

". . . please to hurry," Lisaveta Stepanova was saying urgently into the telephone. "He has a cancer in his brain. . . ."

Although his hands had shaken when it approached the sunflower seeds and although he had jerked the trigger instead of squeezing it evenly, Gregor Mironovich was quite certain the rat was dead, or at least seriously wounded. It appeared to have been a very big rat, although he could not see it clearly due to the poor quality of the American eyeglasses he wore. He was amazed the creature had had the strength to run off.

Gregor Mironovich picked up an empty cartridge from the ground. Laying the rifle on his shoulder, he strolled jauntily out from his hiding place behind the willow, blowing into the shiny brass casing, making it whistle. He would show it to Lisaveta Stepanova and to Christian and his wife so that they would know that with two shots he had either killed the rat or seriously wounded it.

He had quite forgotten about the Americans' crime against him.

But when he reached the door, he found it locked. He knocked, but no one appeared. He called to his wife. She did not answer.

Then he remembered. He felt his hairs stand up like quills. He ran to the kitchen window but could not make out anything through the sheet of plastic. He ran back to the door. He was hammering the rifle butt against it when he saw a blue light come flashing down the dirt road. The light stopped in front of his house and at once was obscured by a cloud of dust, from out of which stepped a tall man in a uniform. Gregor Mironovich could not see his face clearly but as the man stepped forward he saw that his leg, the right one, bowed out.

Gregor Mironovich threw up his hands to surrender. Somehow the rifle went off. The uniformed man leapt behind his car. Gregor Mironovich ran into the woods.

He had not gone far when he stumbled and fell. For a long time he lay on his face on the ground. Each breath sent sharp pains through his chest, his back, and his neck. Gradually, they went away, and his breathing subsided. He smelled the moss and leaves and pine needles beneath him. After a while he was able to stand.

But when he tried to walk his legs wobbled. He collapsed onto the trunk of an uprooted tree. The woods were silent. The only sound was the sound of his breath steaming before him. A few brown leaves, the last remnants of autumn, floated noiselessly down from the trees.

And then he saw the forest in which he was working on the day they had come to arrest him. He had offered no resistance; he had not tried to run away. He remembered it had rained in the night and when he looked back as they led him away, muddy water filled in his footsteps. A mist had lain over the soft ground and the birches had risen from it like ghosts in mourning. They had broken his teeth and sent him away and they had killed them all. His wife had had long hair, thick and dark and wonderful to smell. The baby's fingers, he remembered, had been tiny and perfect.

At the first rustling of leaves, Gregor Mironovich snapped alert. The things he was remembering he blinked away as he might blink away tears. He knelt down behind the tree trunk. He strained to see but could see nothing through the trees. Their black trunks, the brown floor of the forest, the sunless light from the sky blurred into a grayness in which he could distinguish nothing but through which he knew they were advancing.

Raising his rifle, he waited for them to show themselves.